PRAISE

"*Behind the Mirror* illuminates the personal journey to wholeness Julie, the main character, takes as she finds her own path to light. The darkness, challenge, and turmoil she experiences in so many relationships with others turn into lessons, liberation, and triumph as she develops a beautiful bond with the most important person in her life—herself! Bridget Budd deftly weaves together a relatable story layered with humor, humility, and, in the end, a soulful surrender to self-love. A beautiful tale that will empower any woman on their journey within!"

—Dr. Katherine T. Kelly, Licensed Clinical Psychologist

"Budd's unflinching honesty about love, loss, and self-discovery makes this novel both heartbreaking and healing. Raw, real, and ultimately redemptive."

—Kerk Murray, bestselling author of *Since the Day We Danced*

"There comes a point in every woman's life when she must meet herself fully—no longer blaming, no longer bypassing, but choosing radical responsibility, not as punishment, but as liberation. *Behind the Mirror* is an honest and utterly absorbing reflection of that journey. Bridget Budd weaves the delicate lives of her characters into a tapestry so real and raw that I found myself both lost and found in its pages. With raw elegance and deep reverence, Budd seamlessly integrates the potency of Parts Work into the story—offering a portrayal that is resonant, accurate, and profoundly moving. She shows us what becomes possible when we acknowledge, accept, and integrate all parts of who we are. This novel is a luminous invitation to witness the truth beneath the surface. It's messy. It's beautiful. And it leaves you with the quiet peace of knowing: healing is not only possible but waiting for us on the other side of our most honest reckoning."

—Andrea Tessier, M.Ed., Master Life Coach, IFS Practitioner

"This book is a gift for anyone curious and ready to explore the patterns, triggers, and inner struggles that quietly shape our lives. With honesty and compassion, Budd vulnerably guides readers inward, helping them understand how early childhood experiences create survival strategies that once protected us but fuel emotional pain and unhealthy cycles in adulthood. Through Budd's personal journey of self-awareness, growth, and healing, she illuminates a path toward true freedom—reminding us that real happiness is found within ourselves, not in the external world."

—Heidi Carlson, Life Coach & Creator of
The Mother Wound Awakening™

"Reading *Behind the Mirror* felt like hearing a song I didn't know I needed; it's honest, gritty, and healing in all the right places. Bridget Budd doesn't sugarcoat the hard stuff, which makes her story so powerful. As a performer, I often lose focus of the truest version of myself and the version I think people want from me, but then I remember, just like a song, most people want to know that they're not alone, life is messy and not always what it looks like from the outside looking in. This book is a reminder that even when life feels out of tune, there's a deeper harmony waiting if we're brave enough to listen. If you've ever felt lost behind the version of yourself you show the world, this book is for you."

—Erin Viancourt, Nashville Country Music Artist

BEHIND THE MIRROR

Bridget Budd

Print ISBN: 979-8-9990565-1-1

DEDICATION

To all of the beautiful and amazing humans who are unaware that they are already whole, enough, and complete. I see you. I acknowledge you. And I believe in you.

"The most powerful relationship you will ever have is the relationship with yourself."
—Steve Maraboli

ONE

It was an unusually balmy June day in the Pacific Northwest, with blue skies above and billowing clouds in the distance. Laura Carrington, a heavier-set, blonde-haired woman with oversized glasses, walked up the curving entry sidewalk to a beautifully carved set of wooden doors. With a tote bag so massive that her chiropractor should have been on speed dial, Laura touched the bell and tried to stand a little more upright. The large, double brown doors swung open almost immediately, and a petite, slender woman with big blue eyes and an engaging smile said, "Hi Laura, it's so nice to meet you. I'm Julie. Come on in."

Laura, a well-known journalist and Pulitzer Prize winner, often wrote for a national publication in New York City. She was thirty-five when she wrote a groundbreaking exposé on homeless women in Honduras, giving a voice to thousands of displaced people in the country. What makes Laura's accomplishment remarkable is her own journey. Abandoned at eleven years old, she spent most of her adolescence in and out of foster homes—and on the streets. She had a gift for writing, even from a young age, scribbling her earliest essays in the margins of donated books and old scraps of paper. Her raw talent and resilience earned her a full scholarship to Columbia University's School of Journalism. Today, Laura is recognized for her unwavering commitment to truth and justice, often immersing herself for months at a time in the communities she reports on.

As Laura stepped onto the well-worn slate of the foyer, her eyes scanned the room, taking in the expansive space in front of her. Exposed timber trusses offered a sense of warmth to the room, and across the space, several two-story windows framed panoramic views of the water. For a moment, she felt a bit intimidated, but then she remembered why she was there. She recentered herself and said, "Thank you for inviting me, Julie. You have a beautiful home."

Laura came to hear my story, not realizing that every word I spoke would lead me closer to myself.

I smiled genuinely and said, "Thank you. It's been a labor of love." I meant it. I wake up every morning grateful that this is where I get to live. "Follow me out to the deck—that's where the real beauty is." As I led Laura through the house, my exuberantly social chocolate Labrador followed us happily, tail wagging. We stepped onto a weathered mahogany deck, and the vast expanse of the bay spread out before us.

Laura paused for a moment and took in the scenery. "Wow. This is incredible. Living in New York City, my view is nothing like this. Whidbey Island is absolutely beautiful!"

As I began to settle into my favorite comfortable wicker chair, I smiled warmly and said, "Welcome to my little slice of paradise. Come, sit, Laura. Would you like some coffee or some tea?"

"Coffee would be great. Thank you." Laura settled into the chair diagonally across from me. From her behemoth bag, she began pulling out her notebook, writing utensils, and recorder.

She tried to collect the papers that spilled from the bag as a very social and nosy pup sniffed at her ankles.

I thought I'd better make the introduction and said, "This is Lily, by the way. Even at eleven, she insists on being part of every conversation. I hope you don't mind."

Laura scratched Lily behind the ears. "I don't mind at all. She's adorable." After a brief pause, she added, "So Julie, I have to tell you, I didn't really know what to expect for this interview. I learned quite a bit about you while doing my research, and it's amazing to see where you are today. I know a thing or two personally about overcoming adversity. Your life seems rather peaceful and content these days—you seem quite at ease."

"I appreciate hearing that's how you see me. These days, I do feel at ease with myself. Most of the time," I said with a bit of a grin, "I certainly wouldn't be who I am today if I hadn't found the courage to look inward at myself and fully listen to what my life had to teach me. Personal growth and deep soul work can feel like . . . " I paused and continued after finding the words, ". . . like slowly walking barefoot across piping hot coals while wearing a heavy snowsuit during hurricane force winds with the added weight of a one-hundred-and-fifty-pound backpack strapped to your body." I released a long sigh and then continued, "It's not for the faint of heart, but for me, the end result was worth it."

After finishing that statement, I reached over and poured two steaming mugs of coffee from the carafe. The aroma mingled with the salty tang of the sea air. We both had deck blankets draped over the arms of our chairs and wrapped ourselves up loosely to stay warm.

Laura smiled, nodded, and said, "Your analogy is pretty accurate. Looking inward at oneself can be quite humbling. Especially when you do the really deep work." She leaned back in her seat a bit and continued, saying, "I'm excited to hear your story, Julie, and I appreciate you setting aside the next two days for this interview. As I mentioned on the phone, I'm writing a feature called 'Born of Fire: Women Who Give Back, How Trauma Forged Leaders in the Nonprofit World.' When I heard about your story and the organization you created, I knew you'd be a great person to profile. I want my readers to really get a good sense of who Julie Sloan is. Where you grew up, what your home life was like, all the things that make you uniquely you, like having the tenacity to be married four times. I would've given up after two men." Laura raised her eyebrows and chuckled. "Tell me all the stuff I wouldn't ever know about you. You can be as detailed and as intimate as you feel comfortable, Julie."

Laura then hesitated for a moment, her pen poised above the notebook, and continued by saying, "But, first, I want to congratulate you on the National Non-Profit Award your organization won again for the second time in six years. That's remarkable."

"Thank you," I replied with a slight smile. "Girls Rise and Shine means a lot to me, and I know it means a lot to my incredible team and the girls we serve. It's truly an honor."

Laura settled into her seat and turned on her recorder. She gave a thumbs up, indicating the interview was formally starting, and stated, "This is Laura Carrington. Today is day one of my interview with Julie Sloan for the Born of Fire series."

She pushed her glasses back up the bridge of her nose, scribbled two words in her notebook, and confidently asked,

"Julie, can you tell me about your inspiration for the organization and what led you to want to build this type of community? It's really impressive what you and your team have created, and on a national level, no less. Where did the idea for Girls Rise and Shine originate? Was it born from a place of lack in your own life as a young girl? Would you like to start there?"

I sipped my coffee while watching an eagle land, legs outstretched, on a nearby treetop. "To say my life has been full would be an understatement, Laura. When I think back on my life and how I got to where I am today, I'm even amazed." I laughed with a slight snort. "I've never really laid out the full timeline of my life before, but it might be helpful to share the bigger picture so you can understand why I do the work I do with Girls Rise and Shine.

Like all humans, I was shaped by my childhood. How I experienced and interpreted the people and events in my life helped create who I was then and who I am today. None of my experiences were right, wrong, good, or bad—they just were. At a certain point in my life, I had to take responsibility for my beliefs and decisions and begin maturing. I had to figure out what was true for me and not be dependent on what my parents, my friends, or my community thought of me. We all have a story to tell. And if my story invites even just one of your readers to look more honestly at themselves, then it's definitely worth sharing."

Another eagle soared overhead as Laura watched in amazement. "In truth, Laura, I'm in awe of so many things these days. The natural beauty that surrounds me, for starters. The incredible place I get to call home and a loving man who agreed to spend the rest of his life with me. I'm in awe that I get to share this life with my sweet dog, Lily. And even more in awe that I'm still alive, in my late fifties, and trying to live a more self-aware life. The young women who come through our programs are truly inspiring, and I sometimes find it hard to believe that I get to be a part of their lives, as well. They always remind me that my life has come full circle."

I paused and leaned over to give Lily a few long, gentle, sweeping strokes across her head. Lily was chewing on a deer antler, trying vigorously to make a dent in it. I then relaxed back into my seat before continuing. "How about I start at the top with the interesting highlights, and I'll introduce you to Slygore and Athena." I smiled as I watched Laura's face wrinkle with confusion as she raised an eyebrow, her interest clearly piqued.

"I know you did your homework on me, so you are well aware that I am in my fourth marriage. I've been pretty open about that part of my life, but I can usually see people doing the mental math, trying to make sense of it. I get that. However, the truth is that *why* I've been married four times is an essential part of my story.

"What's not so well known about me is that I am estranged from my *mom*, but I've had the privilege of knowing two men whom I called *dad*. Hmmm, let's see, what else? I was kicked out of my house just before tenth grade, and by then, I had already been through four different school systems and lived in as many different cities. I never graduated from college, even though I tried, but somehow, I still managed to earn a lucrative income at a tech start-up company. I was also fortunate enough to leave the workforce at forty-one and create a national non-profit foundation." I paused, then gazed for a moment at Lily sleeping on the deck next to me.

"Laura, if I could invite your readers to take even just one thing from our interview, it would be the idea that looking inward—becoming a self-aware human is worth doing. Most of us seem to investigate the workings of our outer world, yet we seldom learn how to investigate the inner world of our own minds." I placed my hand over my heart and continued, "Is it scary? Absolutely, it is. Learning to pay attention to what's going on deep inside of ourselves takes a lot of courage. It's so much easier to ignore the patterns, beliefs, and behaviors that keep us safe and comfortable in life. The subconscious is a very powerful beast!"

Laura smiled and said, "I can already tell this will be quite an interesting story! Thank you for being so open about your life."

As Laura nestled further into the cozy outdoor chair, I began to dive into my life's story.

Though it took me a really long time—too long, just ask all of my husbands—I'm grateful that I finally decided to look at my life and who I had become. When I started this journey, I wanted to learn about my mind and consciousness, partly so I could finally move beyond the three-year-old tantrums Slygore would throw when he didn't get his way. I wanted to explore behavior patterns, survival strategies, inner child work, boundaries, yoga, spirituality, and countless other modalities. I was eager and pretty ambitious about "fixing" myself.

I knew my early years had affected me, and for the longest time, I struggled to comprehend how my childhood applied to any of those concepts. I had a difficult time connecting the dots. Everything I was learning and trying to embody just seemed like a jumbled mix of concepts and actions. I remember thinking that many of the ideas I explored seemed random and disconnected. I can't tell you how many times I nearly gave up and threw in the towel.

So many questions randomly popped into my head. Did my unreasonableness when someone sat on the edge of a sofa cushion as opposed to the middle of a couch cushion come from some childhood trauma, or was this just an odd quirk of mine? Did I avoid genuinely connecting with people in my younger adult life because I often moved as a child and was forced to navigate new locations and schools constantly? Was my refusal to ask for help my independent personality or a result of mistrust that stemmed from feelings of abandonment by my biological parents? I had so many questions and very few answers.

Slygore and Athena are significant parts of my life for numerous reasons. They are essentially subparts of my personality—and yes, I realize how odd that sounds, so let me explain. In the realm of psychotherapy, the concept of having multiple aspects, or subpersonalities, of oneself in life is not uncommon. Different parts of ourselves can show up to respond to various situations. Learning about this was a particularly important discovery for me because it helped me understand much of my varying thoughts and behaviors in my relationships.

You know that snarky, little voice in your head that shows up just when you're starting to feel a little too hopeful? Well, I call my inner snarky part Slygore. That name seemed fitting for a part of my subconscious brain that reminds me of a creature who slithers around like a fat slug and yells like an ogre. I think of Slygore like a slouch on the couch, making all sorts of demands or saying mean things to me: Bring me that pizza, get me a beer, hand me the remote, you're useless, you're a joke, no one really loves you. He thinks he's doing me a favor when he recites his favorite line at me, "No one loves you. You suck. Go eat worms." Charming, right?

He's not trying to be cruel just for fun. His role is to protect me. Somewhere along the line, he took on the job of keeping people at a distance. He figures if I never let anyone get too close again, I won't get hurt when they eventually leave. He believes that the tough love will harden me up, and I won't fall apart the next time someone walks away. He's mean, but underneath all that bite is fear. And yes, he is exhausting, but I get why he showed up in the first place. He was trying to shield the part of me that's still terrified of being abandoned.

Another more graceful internal voice appeared in my life when I was in my early teens. I call her Athena. Athena is like the calm voice of reason. She is the one who shows up when the chaos dies down enough for me to actually hear her. She's kind, but she doesn't sugarcoat things. She'll call me out gently when I'm spiraling, trying to let me know that I'm not broken, just scared.

Her way of protecting me is by guiding me through the fear, not around it. She's the part that believes in healing and wants me to stop running from everything that hurts. Honestly, she's probably exhausted from watching me listen to Slygore all the time, but she never gives up on me. So, where Slygore thinks abandonment is inevitable, Athena knows it's the fear of it that keeps me stuck.

This is one of the things we teach our Rise and Shine girls. We ask them if they have their own versions of Slygores and Athenas. They usually do, but much of our society just teaches us not to acknowledge those parts of ourselves and to keep them hidden. We help the girls learn that by acknowledging those versions of themselves, they can be powerful allies if they are willing to lean in.

It's fascinating to me how we all embody a strategic self and the true self. The true self is your core essence, representing your inner aspirations, values, and deeply held beliefs. The strategic self does whatever it can to adapt to any situation. It's the version of me who'd show up for this interview fifteen years ago. The one who would be smiling, proclaiming I was happy, and stating that everything in my life was perfect so that you would like me. Finding a balance amid the tension between self-expression and a desire for connection can be incredibly challenging for most people, myself included.

As children, we're wired for attachment. Our survival depends on it—without the support of caregivers and others, we wouldn't have the resources to survive, let alone thrive. Our strategic self helps us adapt to others' expectations and demands and respond to the world around us.

These multiple parts of ourselves highlight certain strengths and downplay weaknesses, ultimately making us chameleons who can adapt to the current situation. While adept at maintaining relationships, these strategic selves often come at the cost of our own sense of identity and inner truth.

Ultimately, without interference, this split between the true self and strategic self becomes internalized, often creating an ongoing conflict in your psyche. The more you prioritize the desires and approval of others, the more disconnected you might feel from your true essence. Over time, it becomes challenging to distinguish what your true self wants versus what your strategic self wants you to want so you'll fit in or gain validation.

After a lot of self-reflection, I was able to see how my strategic self was highly active in most of my relationships. I didn't feel safe to be seen as my true self. This is also very common among many of the girls we see in our programs.

If you really want to get where I'm coming from—and why I started Girls Rise and Shine—it helps to know how I showed up in my own relationships. That part matters.

For a variety of reasons, I have found it extraordinarily challenging throughout most of my life to create healthy, connected relationships where I function well and understand what's happening between myself and the other.

The most significantly challenging relationships for me were my three parents and the four men I married. These seven relationships have contributed to who I am today and my ongoing personal growth. They created room for some pretty profound expansion in my life. At the same time, they've also caused the most pain, shame, grief, and turmoil. I have to say, with gratitude and immense appreciation, that these seven relationships have fundamentally shaped my experience of connection with others. They helped create my core beliefs, and they have been incredibly powerful in showing me what I need to learn in this lifetime.

You see, relationships reflect our own inner world. What we see in others is a reflection of us—like a mirror. We can't see a quality or characteristic we like or dislike in someone unless we feel the same way about it ourselves. People always reflect parts of our consciousness back to us. If we are willing to truly see ourselves and have a willingness to grow and evolve, our relationships can create truly transformational opportunities, helping us shift our beliefs about ourselves and others.

And it's not just enough to look in the mirror. We also have to look behind the mirror if we really want to get to know ourselves at the core. It's like holding up a mirror and realizing, "Oh, this is how I love. This is how I push away. This is how I try to earn worth." The mirror helps us witness our current self—sometimes clearly, sometimes distortedly. It's the inner excavation. The work of self-awareness, shadow integration, and inner child healing. It's not just about seeing the reflection but uncovering what's beneath the behaviors—what's driving them.

For most of my life, I only saw the image of others reflected back to me—versions of who I thought I needed to be to feel loved, safe, and wanted. But, behind every mirror was a lesson, a fracture, a truth I wasn't always ready to face. Each relationship reflected a different aspect—some distorted, some tender, some painfully honest. When I finally stopped adjusting the image and dared to look behind the glass, I found the only thing that had ever been missing: me.

It's taken me a long time to reach a point where I can take responsibility for my part in every one of my relationships. As you might imagine, I didn't exit my three prior marriages with my head held high. I did not uphold my morals and values; that's if I even had any at the time. I can't recall. Most importantly, I've accepted those parts of my life and have forgiven myself. I've learned to let go of the shame, guilt, and unworthiness I carried for way too long. Forgiveness for myself was how I was able to move forward.

As you know, the world is not black and white. How we see it and experience it solely depends on our own perspective and how our brain works. I'm saying this not only because this is the truth from which I'm sharing my story with you, but also to remind you that your perspective can vastly differ from another person's, even during the same encounter.

Remind me to tell you about the rollercoaster experience I had with my mom, Susan. It's a great example of how each person's view of the world is so unique. A person's perspective is essentially a composite of their knowledge, ideas, and beliefs that have been filtered through their specific mental and physical body to become their reality.

Ultimately, what I've gained is empowerment and true freedom. I think empowerment is achieved through self-awareness and by accepting personal responsibility—recognizing who you were, who you are, and how you want to participate in life—and by being free from automatic, deeply ingrained responses. I try to focus on making intentional choices instead of simply reacting to my life with outdated, desperate strategies. It's quite simple in theory, yet incredibly difficult to do.

What I can tell you is that once I decided to honor and live from my true self to the best of my abilities, I was helped along the way by studying the concepts of attachment theory, personality patterns, core human fears, psychosocial development, internal family systems theory, and so many more.

And, rather than try to explain all these theories upfront, if you're interested, I can tell you more about them at the end of our conversation when I talk a little bit about the programs we offer at Girls Rise and Shine. I'd love to see many more young women learning these tools. Not only to benefit themselves but also because when you have and truly embody this type of knowledge, you can positively impact the world!

A beautiful thing happened as I learned more about myself, my gifts, and the things I hid from others. I began to heal and shift my way of being. I saw my life in a whole new way, and my relationship with myself significantly improved. I learned to actually love who I am. Slygore still sits on my couch from time to time, but he is now much less demanding, and Athena talks with me more often. Better yet, my relationships with everyone else in my life became less of a struggle and so much more welcoming.

One of the most important ideas we teach in our community is if—and it's a big if—they decide they want to shift the things that are no longer working for them in their lives or their relationships, then, and only then, do they get to do the work to create change. It is their choice. This is crucial because it seems like nearly everyone these days has an idea or opinion about who I, you, or anyone else should or shouldn't be. And this goes back to perspective and empowerment, right?

TWO

I looked at the empty mug in my hand and then over to Laura. I said, "I don't know about you, Laura, but it's time for me to grab another cup of coffee. Would you like another cup of coffee or anything else to drink?"

"Yes, that would be great. I'd love another coffee. Thank you for asking." Laura answered.

"Okay, just relax and enjoy the view while I pop into the kitchen for a minute." I left the deck with Lily in tow, making my way to the kitchen.

Laura stood, stretched, and wandered over to the railing where she could see the pebbled beach below. Clouds were forming in the distance, and the faint sound of a ship's horn drifted in on the breeze. Ahh, what a place to live. When she saw me return with coffee in hand, Laura took the offered cup and settled back into her seat. I stood at the deck railing for a moment, waiting for Lily to arrange herself in the outdoor dog bed.

Laura smiled and said, "This is delicious coffee! Thank you. I appreciate you sharing so much of your knowledge and details about this part of your life with me. What you shared will be enlightening for my article, and it's also giving me plenty of fodder for my own introspection. This is great stuff, Julie. Before you dive into your relationships, could you provide a little more background about yourself and how you began this journey of self-awareness? Hang on, let me just turn the recorder back on again."

As I sat back down in my chair, I began with the cheeky line I'd used in other interviews. "I've been married for more than thirty years. I just haven't been married to the same man for thirty years." Saying those words and watching the responses of others always made me smile, and Laura's response was no exception. I looked off into the far distance and began my story.

I've been married to four men—all at separate times—for more than a quarter century. And yes, I am currently in my fourth marriage.

However, I have to tell you that I'm in good celebrity company; Elizabeth Taylor, Pamela Anderson, and Christie Brinkley have all been married four or more times. Hubby number four and I have been married for over fifteen years. And so far, we have defied the statistics that say approximately 82 percent of fourth marriages end in divorce. I say approximately because not much research is available on the success of fourth marriages. That's because fourth marriages make up less than 1 percent of marriages worldwide. Does that surprise you? Seriously, how many people do you know who have been married four times—other than me?

You know that old adage about marrying your parent? Well, I think, in my case, I emulated my parents. Stan, who adopted me, Robert, my biological dad, and Susan, my mom, have been married fifteen times between them. Have you heard of Glynn Wolfe?

I saw Laura shaking her head, so I continued. Glynn Wolfe is the world's most married man. He was married thirty-one times to twenty-nine women. All the relationships were monogamous. Can you imagine? I'm more than happy to let Glynn keep that title.

With regard to Robert, Stan, and Susan, I've experienced nine of those marriages personally. I've had six last names since I was born. Susan "kidnapped" me from Robert twice before I was three years old, and when I was fifteen years old, Susan kicked me out of my home.

Here's why this crazy mess is important. This is where those persistent patterns began to take hold. That chaos created a perfect environment for Slygore and Athena. I consistently felt disconnected from others, unwanted, in the way, and not good enough. My life was my life, and it felt normal until one day, it didn't.

While married to Todd—my fourth and current husband—I finally got tired of thinking I was broken. For a long time, I felt something must be inherently wrong with me because not only had I experienced three divorces by the age of forty-one, but I also couldn't recall a time in my life when I felt emotionally close to anyone, not even my parents. I felt zero connection to anyone. Wait, that's not necessarily true. I have always felt a strong connection to animals, but not so much to humans.

The thought of being broken didn't make me feel depressed or angry, nor do I ever recall feeling like a victim in my life. Once I started reflecting on my patterns, I was genuinely inquisitive about why I experienced this emotional distance and why it seemed like I was the only person in the world who felt this way.

Here's an example. For my thirtieth birthday, husband number two, Brian, threw me a fantastic party. He rented a big pavilion at a local beach and hired my favorite local band. He invited about a hundred people. Most of them were his friends or people I knew from work. I didn't really have many friends of my own. A banner that hung at the pavilion entrance said, "Happy Birthday to the Best Wife Ever!" He catered delicious food, and when the night turned dark, he had a few friends create a labyrinth on the beach where beautiful luminaria candles illuminated the walking path.

You'd think I'd be over the moon, thrilled, joyful, grateful, or any other positive emotion you can think of. But mainly, I walked around with a plastic smile on my face. Although everyone thought the smile was genuine, I felt a big, empty void in my heart. I remember Slygore whispering in my ear, *You don't deserve this.*

Athena quietly countered *All of this is for you. You are loved. You are seen. Brian thinks you're amazing.* Who do you think I listened to? Slygore, of course.

I sincerely wanted connection and affection, but those things felt foreign to me. I could say, "I love you," but I had no idea what love and connection should feel like. Was it a jolt? Was it a warm feeling? I honestly didn't know. Inside my body and mind, I felt empty when it came to feeling much. I was pretty numb. And I was excellent at hiding it, I might add.

I married three good men and eventually divorced them because I got in my own way. During each marriage, I had overwhelming feelings of personal dissatisfaction, shame, and lack of worthiness. Unfortunately, the true essence behind the positive emotions I usually conveyed was generally nonexistent. Honestly, I don't know how I lived that way for so long.

I grew up with the fantastical ideology of a "soulmate," which, in my opinion, really undermines the chances of happiness for everyday women because it teaches us to be passive receivers of idyllic romantic expectations. I remember asking myself, *Were those three husbands just not the one? Were they the wrong soulmates?*

When I began to experience the very same desperate feelings of unhappiness in my current marriage, I was somehow dumbfounded. I asked myself, *How in the world am I in the same unhappy situation in my life again? What the hell is wrong with me? Why am I unhappy, unfulfilled, and distant in my relationship again?* It was very frustrating at the time. I did not have the skill set even to begin addressing those questions.

I had and have everything I had dreamed of. This gorgeous house, an indoor pool, a home gym, a massage room, and a state-of-the-art kitchen. Plus, I drive a super fun and sporty Porsche 718 Boxster in Carmine Red, and yes, the irony is not lost on me that I live in Washington and drive a convertible. Nothing beats the top down on the glorious sunny days we have here. Best of all, I am fortunate enough not to have to work for an income any longer. I have the world's best dog, Lily, and great neighbors. I am physically healthy and fit. But I was perpetually unhappy fifteen years ago and had no idea why.

Did you notice that all those things I listed as being everything I dreamed of were external? None of them reflected satisfaction from the inside out. I was living from the outside in. Even as recently as ten years ago, I was stuck in that familiar pattern of thinking that I wasn't worthy whenever Todd, or anyone for that matter, would do something nice for me.

Here's an example. We decided to get new furniture for the living room. I've always been a fan of the sleek Scandinavian design of Jens Ekornes furniture. And let me tell you, nothing is more comfortable to sit in, lounge on, or do whatever else you might imagine. The catch is it's expensive. At least to Slygore, who thought I was still that twenty-something-year-old who scraped by as a lowly office assistant. In my life with Todd, it isn't expensive.

One evening, Todd and I were having a glass of wine out here on the deck, and I broached the subject of getting a suite of Ekornes furniture for the living room. I said, "Honey, I know we've been talking about updating the living room furniture. I've been looking at options and found a wonderful suite with two chairs and a sofa. I love the brand and know you'd love it, too. It might come to about fifteen thousand dollars. What do you think?"

"Babe, if that's what you want, order it."

"But don't you want to see it?" Slygore was beginning to make his voice known.

"I trust you. You have great taste."

Slygore then whispered to me, *I think he's had more to drink than you realize, or he's distracted or something. Todd's not really listening to you.*

So I thought to myself, *Huh, maybe I'm just getting a pacifying answer.* So I said, "Okay, just to be clear, you're really fine with me spending that much on three pieces of furniture?"

"Sure. It's no problem."

Athena kicked in and murmured, *He means it, Julie. It's no problem. He loves you. He wants you to be happy.* But that's not the message I was used to hearing, so I disregarded it.

I said, "Well, if you're not interested in participating in the furniture-buying process, I'll just forget about it." I then got up and walked away.

Yep, I swear to God that conversation actually happened. I asked for something I wanted, was given the go-ahead, and then distrusted the answer so much that I walked away. Who does that? Apparently, me—and I did that for much of my life.

Not long after that conversation, I remember looking out the rain-spattered windows one morning as my brain began to flood me with thoughts of divorce again. I became convinced Todd didn't love me, that he was only pretending, and that I didn't really need him anyway. I wanted to pin my blues on the seasonal affective disorder often felt here in Washington, but I knew if I slowed down enough to look inside, it would be more than that.

This tired, old, negative thought loop went on in my brain for months. Slygore wanted more—more pizza, more beer, more attention, more self-recrimination. He wouldn't shut up. He began taking over more and more of the proverbial couch. It heightened my already existing high-functioning anxiety and was becoming mentally exhausting. Where the heck had Athena gone, and why wasn't she helping me?

One day, I was hiking in the Cascade Mountains, my go-to place to escape it all. I was on a trail dotted with mountain lakes, and I stopped on the shores of one for a bite to eat. It was a glorious sunny summer day, almost hot. Ordinarily, I'm a huge fan of stripping to my undies and jumping in mountain lakes, but for some reason, that day, I was resistant. Maybe I had on saggy underwear; who knows?

As I was lost in a daydream about how miserable I was in my current marriage, a super friendly woman I'd never met before popped her head out of the water and called out to me, "Come on in! The water is cold but refreshing!" She looked so happy bobbing around in the lake, her wet hair sparkling in the sunlight. I could see myself out there on a different day. I still hesitated, thinking to myself, *Gosh, that looks like so much fun. I wish I could do that. I just don't feel like getting wet. All my clothes will stick to me when I get out. Are my undies cute? I already feel crappy, and damp clothes will make it worse.*

Then, as if she could read my mind, she added, "I've got a towel you can use. I'm happy to share!" That did it. She had a nice smile and seemed so welcoming. I realized all I wanted was for someone—a person I didn't know—to be nice to me. I disrobed and hopped in. Damn, that was cold. It was like taking an ice bath. But she was right; it was refreshing. After a few minutes, we couldn't stand the cold anymore, so we waded ashore.

After we got out and dried off, we walked together for a while. We were both hiking solo and going in the same direction. We were both fit and traveled at similar speeds and even had the same boots. She told me her name was Minerva, which I thought was really odd. I'd never met anyone named Minerva before, but I let it go and found I enjoyed spending time in her presence. It was as if just being near her calmed me down and eased my heart and mind.

We chatted a bit about where each of us lived and shared a little bit about our personal lives. I'm fantastic with small talk, so conversation came easily. Then, out of nowhere, she asked, "Have you ever thought about what's real? Are things really real, or do we just think they're real? I mean, describe that tree in front of us. I bet the first things you see about it differ from what I see."

I replied, "I see bark the color of chocolate. It is ridged with deep furrows. I bet it would be a great place for bugs to live. It is about the same height as all the other trees around it."

She countered with, "I see the featheriness of the green needles on long, graceful branches dancing in the breeze. I see the bird sitting more than halfway up. I wonder if it notices I'm here. I see all the other stuff you see, but I see stuff in my own way, too. Does that make sense?"

Intrigued, I nodded.

She continued, "The other day, I read a research study from Stanford University's Wu Tsai Neurosciences Institute. The premise is that you can't always trust that your brain is sending you the correct information."

"What?" I thought this was a bit weird for a conversation with a stranger, but I went along with it.

"It turns out that your brain may unconsciously bend your perception of reality to meet your desires and expectations. It's particularly effective at using past experiences to fill in the gaps when interpreting current situations. They had these cool examples. One of them was a photo of a horizontally striped dress. Apparently, to some people, the stripes are white and gold, while others see them as black and blue. No one really knows why, but the best theory has something to do with whether you're a night owl or an early bird. At any rate, it's fascinating. When you get home, look it up! But essentially, it highlighted that my interpretation of what I'm looking at may not be an accurate perspective at all." Minerva explained.

We walked in comfortable silence for a while. At least to her, I must have seemed silent, but inside my head, I was thinking, *Okay, this is so weird. This woman just gave me the key to unlock the secrets of my mind! If I can't trust my brain's info, is she even real? Did I borrow her towel? Did I jump in the lake? Oh, yep. My wet undies tell me I was in the lake. But it's crazy to think that my brain—or maybe Slygore—is bending reality to meet my expectations of unworthiness. But is it? Maybe my whole life is imaginary. Oh, wait. That's not it.*

After I returned home, I looked up that article. Reading through it helped me realize that I was subconsciously trying to get my needs met in my adult relationships, using the same patterns, beliefs, and behaviors that I had created some fifty years before. Talk about outdated tools! Was it any wonder that I was unhappy in any of my relationships?

I never saw that woman again, but I often think of the lake, her, and the insights she shared with me. I know—at least I think I know—she was a real human. It wasn't until a few years later that I realized Minerva was the Roman name for the Greek goddess Athena. It was no wonder I felt so good in her presence. I've thought about Athena showing up in human form—maybe she'd be like that woman.

THREE

"Laura, do you need a short break before I continue? I need to let Lily out to potty and take a quick break myself. The powder room is just inside and around the corner. If you need anything to eat or drink, our chef, Vincent, can get you whatever you'd like."

"Yes, I do need a quick break as well," replied Laura. She noticed, through the big picture window, that the chef had entered the spacious kitchen and was quietly rummaging through some cabinets. It was late morning by now, and Laura assumed he was preparing lunch for the two of them. Laura was eager to see what the menu would be. A meal prepared by a private chef sounded exciting.

After a brief break, Laura and I returned to the deck, with Lily following closely behind. The clouds had moved off into the distance again, and the sun was now beaming, giving warmth to the day—a rare occasion this time of year. Laura, Lily, and I took a moment to breathe in deeply and feel the sun on our faces.

Laura broke the brief silence and said, "Okay, Julie. The recorder is back on. I'm ready. Let's get back to your story."

Resettling into my chair, I once again looked out into the far distance and gently began the story of Susan, my mom.

I haven't seen or spoken to Susan in nearly thirty years. I removed her from my life because I feared becoming her. I didn't want to live her kind of life. And although I still don't want anything to do with her, I am grateful to her. She gave me life. She didn't have to, and yet, she did. She led a crazy life, at least while I was growing up.

My experience of Susan has varied throughout my life. Sometimes, in my younger years, I felt loved. Often, I felt rejected and misunderstood. Mainly, I felt like a rag doll. Something Susan could put on a shelf and take down to admire, play with, or find comfort in when the timing in life worked for her. I honestly can't remember many good times with her, but I know we had more than a few.

Remember what I shared with you earlier about meeting Minerva and our conversation about perception? Riding rollercoasters is a great example of that! When I was eleven, Susan took me to Elitch Gardens, a local amusement park in Denver. I loved rollercoasters. Or at least I thought I did, though I'd never been on one. I saw the pictures of everyone smiling and screaming, and they looked like they were all having a blast. Maybe I just loved them because Susan loved them, and it seemed like a point of connection. Who knows.

Susan knew how much I wanted to ride the roller coasters, so she stuffed toilet paper into my shoes and told me to stretch as tall as possible to meet the height requirements. It worked— even if, in reality, I was about an inch too short. We waited in line for the cars to come to a stop, and then we got settled into our seats. She helped buckle my seatbelt as tight as it would go, but it was still a little loose. She pulled the safety bar over our laps, and that felt loose, too. But what I didn't know, and what she didn't tell me, was that bracing my feet against the car would help me remain stable.

Up, up, up we went. I was so excited! Then, after cresting the summit, it was all downhill. I screamed, just like the people in the pictures. But I wasn't screaming for joy; I was terrified. Susan laughed and held up her hands, shouting, "This is the best! It's like flying!" She did not seem to notice that I was nearly falling out of the seat and terrified.

We had the exact same experience—same car, same track, same g-force—but she was enthralled, and I was petrified. Once we returned to the loading dock and got out, Susan breathlessly asked if I wanted to get back in line. In response, I threw up. She looked at me coldly and said, "Oh, stop being so dramatic." To Susan's dismay, I begged for tamer rides for the rest of the day.

In truth, I actually do love rollercoasters now that I'm the right size for them. I don't know if this day was an example of excellent parenting, but it is a day I remember and reflect on with a smile.

Susan was born in a small timber town in Montana. She had a brother, Lee, who was one year older. Her half-sister, Anne, was ten years older and from my grandmother's previous marriage. The community where Susan was born and raised is small, straightforward, and honestly seems to be about ten years behind the rest of the world.

Her parents worked in a nearby timber mill for their entire marriage until they retired. During my high school years, I lived with my grandparents, but I was too preoccupied with my own desperate teenage drama to be involved in their lives in any meaningful way.

My grandmother, Sarah, Susan's mom, had an entire life before meeting my grandfather. She was married at a young age and was divorced when she met him. Divorcing in the late 1940s wasn't common, especially for the woman to initiate. My family never talked about her prior marriage. Susan's half-sister, Anne, was the only reminder of my grandmother's previous life. Sarah was a quiet, heavy-set woman with curly blonde hair. She was a people pleaser, very loving and yet quite stoic at the same time. She passed away when I was about twenty years old. She had a sudden heart attack and didn't even make it to the hospital. Regrettably, I didn't go to her funeral.

Susan's dad, Jack, was a loving man as well. He was thin, active, and rigid in his daily routine. He was a decorated Army veteran who received numerous awards and medals from World War II while serving in the Philippines and Japan. He was a prisoner of war (POW) and received a Purple Heart. When he passed away in the late 1990s, I did attend his funeral. A three-gun salute and flag-folding ceremony honored his service to his country. It was a somber yet beautiful tribute.

My grandparents were warm and attentive to my many cousins and me. They spent time with us, entertained us, fed us, and took us on vacations. They seemed like wonderful grandparents to me. I'm not sure about their parenting skills, though. I don't think they were as loving to their children as they were to their grandchildren. Not intentionally, but simply because of their generation. I never got the impression they were as attentive as parents. I've often wondered if Susan would have turned out differently if they had been. You know, nature versus nurture.

In the 1940s and 1950s, I imagine that tending to the emotional needs of children was far less prevalent than it is today, or even in the 1970s and 1980s when I was young. I'm inclined to believe that Susan's parents were much more hands-off—especially if a child or children might have been an embarrassment in a small conservative timber town.

I've seen pictures of Susan, and she was a beautiful child. Her heart-shaped face offered a mischievous smile, and her bright blue eyes were framed by thick red hair. She was always petite but strong, both in body and temperament. And according to Susan herself, she mastered the skill of manipulation at an early age. Apparently, she knew exactly how to cock her head and smile or pout to get precisely what she wanted.

I think she felt like the only attention she received was from people who wanted something from her. We've never talked about this; it's just something I've sensed. I grew up feeling invisible. I can't imagine what life would have been like for Susan during the age of free love, as everyone always noticed when she walked into a room.

Though I don't know many stories about Susan's early life, according to several relatives in her family, as a teen, Susan loved using acid—some people call it LSD. Though it seems astonishing to me, acid was legal for years and wasn't considered a Schedule I drug until the fall of 1968. Even after it became illegal, it wasn't hard to get for those who knew where to find it. I suppose when you get hooked on a drug—a legal drug, no less—in your early teens, you find a way to keep up with it as time passes, right?

Maybe her affection for acid, pot, and alcohol was a way to hide the thought that everyone wanted something from her. She never told me of any experiences of sexual assault. But as pretty and precocious as she was, I'd be surprised if she didn't have unwanted sexual encounters. Maybe in the 1960s, unwanted advances weren't considered assault; they were just part of the social perspective about sexuality and relationships. I have no idea.

During their teenage years, Lee, Susan's brother, was into drugs and alcohol, too. Apparently, if anyone in town during those days wanted drugs, they went to Lee and Susan. I discovered this only because while I was a teen living with my grandparents, some of my friends' parents didn't want me around their kids. When I told them I was living with my grandparents because Susan kicked me out of my house and didn't want me anymore, they were a bit more forgiving.

During Susan's high school years, she had a reputation for "negatively" influencing many of her classmates. And yes, I did just gesture air quotes when I said the word negatively. I wish I knew what beliefs Susan had formed about herself at that age. Did she have any values? Who was influencing her? Did she have any dreams of who she wanted to be in life? It's one of those things I've stopped trying to figure out. Her older sister Anne had already left home by then, and I doubt she had many other positive influences in her life. I often see this with the girls we support. They don't have many healthy, involved role models helping to guide them. Many of these girls live lives that mirror Susan's.

In 1965, Susan was seventeen when she dropped out of high school to marry her high school sweetheart, Chip. And no, she wasn't pregnant, but I can only imagine that wearing the labels of a druggie and a promiscuous woman helped cement the decision to drop out of high school. Susan once told me the story of how she threw a big enough temper tantrum that her parents canceled their vacation plans for that summer and gave her the money for her wedding.

She told them if they didn't let her marry and pay for the wedding, she'd never speak to them again. Honestly, if she were my daughter, I think I would have said, "Well, Susan, finish school and stay, or pack your bags and move on. I'm not willing to be held hostage." My grandparents apparently were not good disciplinarians. Perhaps Susan acted the way she did because her parents didn't set any boundaries with her. Or, maybe they tried to invoke rules with her, and she ignored them anyway. Who knows. I felt such sadness for her and my grandparents when Susan shared that story with me. What chaos her life must have been.

A few years ago, when I was thinking about Susan and what might have given her reason to get out of the house at such a young age. I came across a website that said that 42 percent of first-time brides in 1965 were under the age of twenty. Clearly, getting married at seventeen was not as big of a deal back then.

I never asked her what was so appealing about marriage or Chip that made her force my grandparents to give their consent. She wasn't pregnant, so was she running to or away from something? Did my grandparents even care that she dropped out of high school? Maybe escapism was a way to hide some deep sense of unworthiness. I don't know.

Susan and Chip stayed married for about two years. In 1966, the draft was in full swing, and Chip was called up. He was shipped out to South Vietnam within a year of marrying Susan. While he was overseas serving his country, Susan said he didn't write home enough, and she lost interest in him. That's when she began a relationship with Robert—my biological dad.

She was nineteen years old and volunteering at a hospital when she got pregnant with me in late 1967. Once she knew she was pregnant, she filed for a no-fault divorce from Chip and married Robert, who worked in his dad's machine repair shop. Five months later, Chip was killed in action. She never really talked much about him or their relationship.

Being pregnant, recently divorced, and looking for the next man to save her, I can see why my dad, Robert, fit that bill. He told me once that I most likely saved Susan's life. When she got pregnant, she had to make one of several choices: give up her drug use to have a healthy child, continue the drug use and give birth to, in all likelihood, a mentally and or physically disabled child, or have an abortion, which was illegal at that time. Robert told me Susan contemplated abortion, but, for whatever reason, chose to quit her drug habit while she was pregnant. Maybe getting a back-street illegal abortion was more terrifying than giving up the acid? Neither choice was likely an easy one for her.

Though I don't have anything to do with Susan these days, I'm incredibly grateful she decided to give birth to me. I'm also thankful that she didn't pick her drug and alcohol habit up again until after she was done breastfeeding.

For as long as I can remember, though, I've felt an odd coldness or maybe resentment Susan has towards me, yet I could never really pinpoint the reason. I've often wondered if it's because having me forced her to stay off drugs for a period of time. I've never been addicted to drugs or alcohol—thank goodness. I do have a pretty serious dark chocolate addiction, so I imagine how difficult it was for her to temporarily give up her acid habit. Unfortunately, as soon as she could, she plugged right back into what was left of the local hippie culture—she made peace, love, and fun her main priority again.

Most of the time, we can't see the patterns forming in our lives until we are deep in them or want to change them. We just think it's our personality or the "way we are." By this time in her life, Susan had already developed a tendency to flee when things were tough or not going according to her expectations.

I can't even imagine what Susan was feeling when I came into the world in early August 1968. She was young, living in a rural small town, had an infant and a second husband, and was trying to obtain her GED—an alternative to a high school diploma. College was probably never a real option for her, and if she hadn't left town, she likely would have ended up at the sawmill, tending bar, or becoming a housewife. I don't know what her aspirations were as a teenager, but I doubt the life she had was what she had envisioned. Or maybe she never allowed herself to have big ideas or thoughts on her path in life. Maybe all she could see was her life in that small town. With me now in her life, whatever dreams she had, whoever she wanted to become, she'd have to work that much harder to obtain them.

At some point in 1969, when I was a little over a year old, Susan and my biological dad, Robert, split up. Robert stayed put, and Susan just up and disappeared, or so I've been told. Robert knew she was alive only when the divorce papers landed in his lap. Susan was twenty-one years old and was now on the path to her second divorce. Within the year, Robert gained full custody of me because Susan failed to show up to one—or several—court custody hearings. I never got an answer as to what was so important to her on the day of the custody hearing that she'd choose to miss it. But something more important that day kept her from being present.

Over the years, I've tried to imagine myself as a toddler. I've always been curious as to what I was learning about the world around me. What behaviors was I already developing? What patterns had already been put into motion for Slygore to latch onto and cultivate? How might Athena have been protecting me even though I didn't know it?

I know children begin forming special bonds with their caregivers during the first years of life, so what did Susan's abandonment mean to me regarding the ability to create deep attachment, trust, and strong relationships? At that age, I would have been trying to develop a sense of being nurtured and loved and potentially more complex emotions like separation anxiety. That little girl version of me must have felt confused and sad without her mom. I'm really glad I don't have any conscious memories of that time in life.

In 1970, while Robert still had full custody of me, Susan popped back into town a few times. On two of those occasions, without permission from the courts or Robert, she whisked me off to Denver to "spend some girl time." Which sounds strange, right? What twenty-two-year-old calls time away with her toddler "girl time?" The first visit was for a week, and the second visit became permanent.

She chose Denver for our girls' trips because she had somehow formed a relationship with a wonderfully mature guy with a stable career as a traveling salesman. His name was Stan, and he was fourteen years older than Susan. He never bought into the hippie, drug, free-love culture. He was a pretty straight-and-narrow kind of guy, and he still is. To this day, I have no idea what Stan saw in Susan. Maybe she offered a peek into a different world. Maybe her beauty and precociousness were infectious.

Maybe it was me. By the second visit, Stan adored me, and he loved the idea of having a daughter—this gave Susan bonus points. She never returned me to Robert, and Robert's repeated efforts to bring me back home ultimately failed. Within that year, Susan turned twenty-three and entered her third marriage with Stan.

Right after she married Stan, Susan got a lawyer and filed for custody of me. After two years of attorneys and court appearances, I was four years old when Susan gained sole custody of me. By then, Robert had failed to respond to any of the correspondence sent to him by the Colorado court system, and he had repeatedly ignored the court's requests for appearances. Robert gave up fighting for me. Susan could certainly be cutthroat when she wanted to gain the upper hand. I speculate that getting custody of me was more about punishing Robert—for what I'll never know—and less about regaining her daughter.

Once Susan gained custody of me, she and Stan petitioned the court to allow Stan to adopt me. In October of 1973, I was just over five when the paperwork was completed, and Stan officially adopted me. Per the courts, I had been officially abandoned by my biological father.

Imagine hearing when you're five that your dad has abandoned you. I don't think I was meant to hear them talking about it, but little ears hear all kinds of things. Including things they don't understand, so they interpret them in their own ways. Did my five-year-old self begin to think I was unlovable? Would he ever come back for me? Susan left me for a period of time, and now the only dad I'd ever known had done the very same thing.

Susan, Stan, and I lived in Denver until 1978, when Susan decided she was done with Stan and all his traveling and asked for a separation and divorce.

It was early summer, and I'd just gotten out of sixth grade. I really loved my elementary school. It was three blocks from home and next door to a great park with a long grassy hill. In the summer, I would roll down the hill like a log, laughing the entire way, and in the winter, when it was snowy, the hill was perfect for sledding.

I excelled as a student in elementary school. I liked most of my teachers and spent many happy afternoons helping out after class. I'd sweep the floors, erase the chalkboards, clean the counters, and do anything else asked of me. Getting the candy bar as payment was only part of the reason I did it—hence the chocolate habit I now have. I think I realized by then that staying late at school was a safe and happy place for me to spend time and where I was nurtured. I didn't feel that way at home with Susan while Stan was on the road, but I wouldn't have been able to identify that at that time.

Being around Susan never felt comfortable for me. I loved her, but she didn't exactly radiate maternal energy. And without Stan's influence, home didn't feel the same.

When Susan and Stan separated, Susan took me to San Francisco, California. It turns out she'd met a man, Marc, at a bar in Denver who was still connected to the fading hippie scene, and she longed for those days. He had an apartment in the Haight, and there were a couple of kids my age who lived next door, Jenny and Peter.

San Francisco differed vastly from small-town Montana or Denver, especially the Haight-Ashbury neighborhood. At first, the adventure was intoxicating for an eleven-year-old. On weekdays, the sidewalks were crowded with rebels and long-haired hippies sitting around either smoking dope or asking for change so they could buy dope. The weekends turned the streets into an overwhelming combination of street fair, costume ball, and circus, with Krishna devotees everywhere. Whenever I smell patchouli, vivid memories of those crowded streets flood back into my brain.

Susan and Marc stayed out all hours of the day and night. It was as if I didn't even exist. If they did come back to the apartment, they often brought people with them. I felt lucky that I had a tiny bedroom to escape into where I could close the door. Many mornings, I'd emerge from my room and find strangers passed out on the floor. Looking back on it later, it felt like I was playing a live version of Frogger as I hopped over people, making my way to the kitchen.

I spent as much time with Jenny and Peter as possible, but their home life wasn't much better. All of our parents had odd jobs and found the nightlife more rewarding than raising kids. For most of that summer, the three of us would go into local sundry shops and steal trinkets, which we would then sell to tourists. For the record, I am not proud of this behavior, but often, our parents were too busy working, partying, or too hungover to buy food, so our entrepreneurialism ensured we had food in our bellies.

I don't remember exactly how it happened, but I ended up registering for junior high alongside Jenny and Peter. Their mom had enough of her wits about her to take them and agreed to let me come along. If I hadn't gone with them, I think Susan would have completely forgotten I was supposed to be in school.

School was the one place where I had structure and routine, something I very much needed in my life, and it was a place where I could be a kid. I was constantly being put in adult situations that were developmentally inappropriate for me. I was way too young to have those responsibilities.

Stan called to check in on me every other week. He was still legally my dad but didn't fight Susan for custody. They agreed to some type of visitation, but while we lived in San Francisco, we only got to talk on the phone. He would always tell me he loved me, and I would always tell him I was fine and having fun.

Stan is the first person I remember intentionally lying to. I told him what he wanted to hear rather than being honest with what I felt inside. He wanted to visit me a few times, but I felt ashamed of how Susan and I were living our lives, and Susan was very adamant about Stan not coming to San Francisco.

Once school started, I felt pretty disconnected from everything. Yes, Jennie and Peter were there, but they had their own friends. I just couldn't seem to find my way. The teachers were stoic and less caring. And the way we shuffled around from room to room for class was very different from elementary school. I just wanted to feel at ease, but I felt like I was always on edge, waiting for the next thing to happen.

That January, the next thing did happen. It was a rainy afternoon, and I had just gotten home from school. I unlocked the apartment door and walked in. I felt a chill in the air and intuitively sensed something was wrong. Though I didn't call her Athena then, I remember a soft, kind voice whispering to me, *Don't worry. It will be okay. Remember to breathe. You'll be okay.* I shook my head to clear the voice and looked at my surroundings more closely.

Our luggage was packed and sitting next to the door. Susan came out of her bedroom crying. She seemed astonishingly sober, which worried me even more.

I said, "Mom, what's going on?"

"We're leaving."

"Why?"

"Marc's an asshole."

"What? Why. What is going on?"

"He's decided he wants back with his ex-girlfriend, and he's kicking us out. We have to leave today."

"What? That's crazy! What are we going to do? I have school tomorrow."

She took a deep breath and said, "I called Stan. He booked airline tickets for us, and we're leaving for the airport now. We are going back to Denver to live with him again." I was so glad my calm inner voice told me to breathe and that I'd be okay.

I asked Susan if I could say goodbye to Jennie and Peter, and she abruptly told me no. I was heartbroken. I had spent so much time with Jennie and Peter all those months, and to not even be allowed to say goodbye was devastating. I couldn't believe this was happening again. She grabbed my hand and pulled me out of the apartment. When we got to the sidewalk, she hailed a cab that took us to the airport.

I have no idea if she even called the school to let them know I was leaving. We'd only been in San Francisco seven months, and now we were going back to Stan in Denver. In a matter of a few hours, I lost my best friends, my home, and my school. And sure, I was going back to live with Stan and back to a place I loved, but my body was overwhelmed with emotion. I remember feeling very edgy and tense about the whole situation.

Susan and Stan remarried within a couple of months of our return to Denver. Even now, I'm astonished that he was willing to let her go, let alone take her back so easily. Maybe he was excellent at accepting her just as she was. I certainly never could. To Stan's surprise, but not mine, Susan was ready to move on again within the year. She filed for yet another divorce at the end of my seventh-grade year.

This time, Susan moved us to Durango, Colorado, where she picked up a job serving drinks at the local bar. She and I lived in a tiny apartment above a flower shop. At this point in my life, I had begun to numb out. If I felt any emotion at all, I buried it, thinking no one cared how I felt anyway. I remember very little of my life in those years. I have virtually no memories of the friends I made, the things I did, or the places I went. I do remember the first boy who kissed me, though I can't recall his name. However, the smell of fresh-cut flowers drifting up from the flower shop below is something I distinctly remember. The smell always made our little home smell like a booming garden.

I also remember that Susan and I were very poor after she and Stan divorced. We didn't have much in terms of material things, but at the same time, my life was less tumultuous. Susan was relatively drama-free, except for the morning her car got repossessed by the bank, and I couldn't get to school. Susan was so embarrassed that she told everyone, even the police, that her car had been stolen. I perpetuated that story when the school asked why I had been absent for a few days. It was easier than making Susan out to be a liar.

Scouring the couch cushions, dresser drawers, and Susan's closet for loose change became an interesting game I played when I wanted to scrape up enough money for ice cream at the cafe directly across from our apartment. I was there so often that the employees sometimes let it slide if I was short on cash. It was seriously some of the best ice cream I've ever had.

I'm not sure what it was about living in Durango, but I did enjoy my time there. I can't identify it, but something about the place put me at ease. Maybe it was the mountain air? It might have been the trees, or wildlife, or the local river running through town. Perhaps it unconsciously reminded me of Montana, where I spent my toddler years.

Susan dated quite a few men after divorcing Stan. It seemed as if she was in the shopping mall trying to find a new blouse. She'd try one man on, and if he didn't suit her, she'd cast him aside and try the next one. A string of men wanted to date and claim the beautiful, mischievous Susan. Eventually, she settled on a man named Roger, a forty-something, childless bachelor who ran a small ranch outside Salem, Oregon.

Rodger came into town for some spring skiing and stopped in each night at the bar where Susan worked. Susan, with her blue eyes and red hair, must have cocked her head in just the right way to keep him coming back. Rodger was a big tipper, and this immediately captured Susan's attention.

After he returned home to Oregon, Rodger stayed in touch. At the end of my eighth-grade year, Roger proposed to Susan, and we headed off to Oregon. Without so much as an introduction to the man, I was moving yet again to meet and live with my new stepdad.

Before meeting him, I assumed Roger had money and that his ranch was pretty big; otherwise, why would Susan have uprooted me again from another school? However, looking back on it, I don't believe Susan even considered that I might need some long-term stability in my life. I'm pretty sure she didn't even check out the neighborhood or school system before deciding to move us to Oregon. Roger's offer to marry her carried more weight than providing me with much-needed permanence.

For the first time in my life, moving felt awful, painful even. I had moved so many times before, but this move was different. Our life in Durango finally felt like a place to call home, even if I was there for only a year. Susan seemed a little nicer to me, and she was together enough to keep food in the fridge. We even watched TV together on the weekends. It felt nice for a change.

Back then, I never understood why Susan thought she couldn't stand on her own two feet, why she felt like she needed a man to be happy. Although she was beautiful on the outside, she lacked self-awareness and confidence on the inside. She relied solely on men to make her feel whole.

In my maternal line, the urge to marry and a deep-seated feeling of unworthiness are generational traits. Like many families, mine carries inherited patterns of behavior, beliefs, and coping mechanisms that have been passed down through generations. These patterns often emerged as survival strategies in response to real or perceived trauma. In my family of origin, the women were taught—sometimes subtly, sometimes overtly—that to feel whole, a man had to be present. From a young age, most women of my generation and those before me were conditioned to believe that men were essential for our sense of security and companionship.

I shared earlier that my grandmother had been married before marrying my grandfather. I imagine she must have carried some guilt, shame, and feelings of unworthiness from initiating a divorce in that era. Recent scientific research on epigenetics suggests that trauma, like in the case of my grandmother's divorce—and the intense emotions that came with it—can be passed down on a genetic level. That would explain, in part, some of Susan's own behavior patterns or why she would experience similar emotions. Or maybe it's just purely coincidental that on my maternal side of the family, my grandmother was married twice, Susan has been married five times, and I've been married four times. We would certainly make a great case study!

Susan, Rodger, and I lived in Oregon during my ninth-grade year. Rodger's house was on a ranch a few miles from town, and no other families were close by. At first, it seemed like an absolutely boring place with very little to do for someone my age. I spent most of my time in my bedroom, which was a converted guest room with dark green paint and a big picture window, or exploring the massive property with Rodger's two ranch dogs, Moose and Bear. Those two silly mutts became my best friends and confidants.

I came to love walking out in the fields with Moose and Bear by my side. When we arrived in the late summer, the leaves on the maples and alders turned beautiful shades of orange and yellow. Around the house, I'd rake them into piles for burning, but often, before Rodger had a chance to start the fire, the black feral barn cat would rustle through them as if it were the best game on earth.

As for school, I was starting the year again, knowing no one. I did my best to stay out of sight and keep a low profile. Long gone was the happy and eager elementary school kid who couldn't wait to help out after class. Most days, I felt invisible at school and home, and I did nothing to change that. The last thing I wanted to do was actually like Roger, make friends, and really enjoy living on that ranch. Slygore was constantly telling me that it was just a matter of time before Susan up and moved us again, probably for another new man.

On cold, snowy days in the winter, if the wind kicked in, the snow would blow across the fields, almost looking like ocean spray. Winter had a totally different smell than fall. It was fresh and sharp and seemed like steel. In the winter, I liked going into the barn to do my homework in the hayloft. Even though it was cold outside, the barn always seemed cozy and warm. Rodger installed stairs to the loft rather than a ladder, so Moose and Bear could climb up and lounge beside me in the dusty air while I studied.

By spring, Susan was starting to go a little stir-crazy out on the ranch. She was naturally social, and the quiet, isolated life away from town simply didn't give her the stimulation she craved. Her need for male attention—and the insecurity driving it—was becoming more obvious by the day. Even though it seemed clear to me that Roger loved her, I'm not sure she ever truly felt it. She started cracking open the vodka bottle around noon and slowly drinking her way through the day. Occasionally, she'd ask me about school, but most of the time, she left me alone. Even though I was on my own most of the time and didn't have many friends at school, I was actually beginning to feel comfortable in Oregon.

Spring brought the bubbling creek to life, and the flowering trees opened their blossoms to the sky. I loved watching all the new growth pushing up out of the ground or bursting out from branches. The ewes had their lambs, and they were so cute as they bounced around on their skinny legs, bawling for their mamas.

I appreciated that Rodger showed me things and talked with me about the seasons on the ranch. With Susan in the bottle every day and incoherent most of the time, Rodger started spending more time with me, showing me how to repair things on the ranch, teaching me how to care for the animals, and how to navigate the land with a compass. It was fun to have a father figure in my life again. I missed Stan, and even though we talked on the phone every other week, I missed his presence. I missed having my dad around. And just like Stan, Rodger represented stability and predictability but in a more grounded and earthy way.

Then, one June morning, shortly after school was out for the summer, out of the blue, Susan stormed into the barn where I was playing with the dogs and screamed, "I'm shipping you off to your grandparents' house in Montana. I don't want you coming back here."

I was stunned. Before I could stop myself, I blurted out, "Why? I like it here. What did I do wrong?"

Slygore was shouting as well, telling me how much Susan hated me and that if I were a better person, this wouldn't keep happening to me.

"You've been spending way too much time with Rodger, and I don't like it."

What? That calm, quiet voice that I'd now named Athena popped into my head, saying, *Don't worry. It will be okay. Remember to breathe. You'll be okay.* "Mom, what are you talking about? Rodger is just being nice to me. He tells me about the ranch and teaches me stuff. That's all."

"He's too nice to you. He needs to spend more time with me."

I had a million unkind things I wanted to shout right back at her, but instead, I hesitated. In that moment, I unexpectedly saw clearly how Susan craved attention yet pushed people away. She wanted love, but she sabotaged every relationship, especially her relationship with me.

I shouted, "If you'd just be nicer to him and weren't drunk all the time, he'd probably want to spend more time with you." Uh oh. Where did that come from? I learned early in my life never to talk back to Susan. The consequences were never good. I ran around the back side of some hay bales.

She lunged at me and tried to grab my hair. "You're nothing but a little whore. All you want is for my men to like you! You flirt with all of them. Men always want the teenage girls. You're the problem. You're the one who has destroyed all of my marriages. I want you out of here. Rodger is mine. I don't want to see you again—ever."

I tried to remember to breathe, but I was petrified. At this point, I was cowering, and she had stopped lunging at me. Again, I heard Athena's voice whispering, *This isn't about you. It's about her. She needs help, and this is not your fault.* The fact that Susan would think I would try to take her husband away from her sounded so gross to me at the time. My head was spinning.

I bolted out of the barn and found Rodger near the house. At that point, he was my safety net. I told him what Susan just said to me. I wanted him to back me up. Although life wasn't great, it wasn't all bad, and I did not want to move again. Unfortunately, he just held up his hands, shook his head, and said, "Sorry, kid. You know what your mom is like. Nothing I can do about it."

I remember feeling confused and exhausted. *Abandoned again*, Slygore chanted. He then whispered, *This is your fault. You're worthless. No one wants you. No one cares.* I ran to my room and slammed the door. I thought to myself that Athena was wrong this time; things would not be okay.

Feeling displaced again created an emotional numbness throughout my entire body. I just wanted to shut down and tune it all out. The following couple of days were just as terrible. I tried to avoid Susan and Rodger and went for long walks with the dogs. I was heartbroken knowing I had to leave Moose and Bear. Tears freely rolled down my face. I told them everything that was on my mind and in my heart. I knew they understood because they looked sad and kept pressing up against me.

Two days later, Susan put me on a bus back to Montana. Slygore was right; it was just a matter of time before I had to move again. Only this time, I was alone. With my three small suitcases in tow, twenty dollars in my pocket, and a half-eaten bag of snacks, I arrived at the bus station in Montana. My grandparents cheerfully greeted me as I walked off that bus fourteen long hours after leaving Oregon. Susan never once came to visit me.

Susan's marriage to Roger lasted four more years until she again divorced—for the fourth time. Roger wasn't a bad guy.

He just had no idea what he was getting into when he married Susan. Though I hadn't been around for years when she divorced Roger, she found some way to blame me as the cause of that failed marriage. That didn't surprise me.

Accountability was never Susan's strong suit. I never knew if her early drug use did something to her brain or if she simply lacked emotional maturity. Back then, she certainly didn't have a sense of self-reflection, self-awareness, or desire to shift any of her damaging patterns or beliefs. However, as I mentioned, I haven't been in contact with her for more than thirty years. Maybe she's changed?

A few years later, after divorcing Roger, Susan married another man, Grant. From what I have heard from others, Susan and Grant are still married. I don't recall how they met or many of the details of their marriage. Grant seems to love her for exactly who she is. He continuously supports her and stands by her side no matter what she does. If she is happy and content with her life, then I am genuinely happy for her. We all deserve happiness, love, and freedom from the things that hold us back in life. And we all deserve to have people in our lives who love us for who we are—not for who they want us to be.

About twenty-five years ago, I finally chose to sever my relationship with Susan. I did this for my own mental well-being and because I needed a clear boundary with her. She's tried to contact me several times since by mail. While I appreciate the effort, Susan lacks the capacity for self-reflection and self-awareness, which makes it impossible for me to have any kind of relationship with her. There's a silence that only a mother can leave behind. Mine wasn't marked by absence alone—but by presence without warmth, love with strings, and the ache of wondering what I did wrong.

My lack of relationship with Susan is not a matter of forgiveness. I have forgiven her. Instead, my choice has more to do with my deep knowledge of myself and the type of people I want in my life. I am taking care of that little girl inside me now. I am protecting her.

I stopped responding to Susan's letters decades ago. They inevitably expressed her limited perspective in life. Some of the letters proclaimed that I didn't care about her. Others highlighted her various health issues, included random pictures of her home, or blamed me for something I did to her when I was fourteen years old. Her true intent behind sending me letters was always unclear to me. I believe that Susan is frustrated and venting her feelings in the only way she can.

What I often tell my family when Susan's name comes up in conversation is that Susan is consistently Susan. I can depend on that, and I have been able to accept that about her.

In all likelihood, Susan doesn't hate me or even dislike me. I believe that she was, and perhaps still is, struggling to cope with her own issues and maybe even her own intergenerational trauma. She has mentally rewritten the story of my childhood to protect herself. From what I imagine her perspective to be, I can see why she would do that. Acknowledging the truth of how she discarded and abandoned me would mean facing the truth of what she did. I believe she would prefer to live in denial than do the uncomfortable and challenging work of taking accountability. Facing yourself fully—the light and the shadow—is not for the faint of heart.

FOUR

Laura took a deep breath, glanced out at the water, and paused before acknowledging what I had just shared with her. "Wow, Julie. I can only imagine what it must have felt like to have that experience of your mom."

I replied, "Yes, it is a lot to take in. Thank you for listening so intently. Also, here's one last thing. For the most part, I'll intentionally try to leave Susan out of the rest of our interview because I don't want to distract from what I'll share about my relationships with Stan, Robert, David, Brian, Andy, and Todd. Ultimately, her later life interferences are irrelevant to the story of my life."

Laura stretched, then said, "I'm starting to see why you're not only estranged from her but why you feel so drawn to helping other young women. I've interviewed many people in my career, and it's always been interesting to learn how their upbringing impacted their adult lives. It's so fascinating. Have you ever thought of writing a memoir?"

I pondered Laura's question, and before responding, I leaned over to give Lily a soft kiss on top of her big furry head. "You know, I've never really given it much consideration. Maybe I will someday."

Chef Vincent walked onto the deck and gently signaled to us that lunch was ready to be served. Laura was eager to stand up for a bit, and as she rose from her chair, she also noticed that her stomach was rumbling quite loudly. Lily then sprang to her feet as well, rushed past Laura, and bolted over to greet Chef Vincent. With a few eager wags, Lily trotted after him through the double doors and into the house.

As I headed toward the doors, I said, "I'm starving. Let's make our way to the kitchen."

Laura was glad not to be the only one in need of food at the moment. As they walked into the house, the scent of freshly baked bread filled the air, mingling with the aroma of wild-caught salmon roasting. I escorted Laura to the long reclaimed wood table placed off to the side of the kitchen by a massive bay window. The kitchen sprawls across nearly half the main floor. It's huge.

Laura thought to herself, *This isn't your average cooking space. It looks like a commercial kitchen, the most elegant I've ever seen.*

Lily was already at her feeding mat, devouring the salmon garden bowl Chef Vincent had prepared for her. On the counter, a special plate of homemade natural peanut butter and apple treats waited for his favorite furry pal when she finished her lunch. He loved that dog. He often joked with me that he might steal her one day.

Laura and I sat opposite each other at the large table, which was adorned with dishes in a deep orange chinoiserie style. We began to converse over our carefully designed meal, which included chilled cucumber and avocado soup, roasted salmon served over a warm quinoa and roasted vegetable salad, accompanied by shaved fennel and apple slaw. As we talked and ate, we discussed Laura's career and her family life, shared stories about pets, and chatted about upcoming vacations.

Above all else, we recognized how much wiser we both felt as we aged. It was delightful to see how much we had in common. I realized how much I liked Laura, and I could see us becoming good friends.

When we finished lunch, I decided that my home office would be a better place to continue our conversation as a light drizzle set in, so we headed over to the opposite side of the house. We settled into tan leather chairs, which hugged another massive two-story, floor-to-ceiling window with sweeping outdoor views. The cozy, well-organized room featured walls covered in grass-cloth wallpaper featuring botanicals and birds. The walls looked almost magical. Bookshelves, which housed thousands of books, were placed strategically. I noticed Laura scanning all of the titles. With a big grin, I said, "I know. I have a lot of books. You'd never guess that reading was a recently discovered hobby of mine, would you?"

Laura smiled and politely said, "No, not at all. It's quite the collection you have here."

Chef Vincent brought us cups of warm tea and placed a large tray of assorted, freshly made desserts on a credenza. Laura pulled her notebook and pen out of her voluminous bag and started her recorder again. I took a sip of tea, nodded to Laura, and said, "Let me tell you about Robert."

Robert was my biological father. He and his family cared for me during my infancy. They also looked after me when we reconnected in my late teenage years. Robert was a quiet contradiction—kind and loving yet somewhat distant. He had a gentleness about him but also a certain emotional detachment I could never quite figure out.

He was tall and slender but strong, had a short mop of sandy brown hair, an easy smile, and warm, golden-brown eyes. He carried a quiet charm, especially with women. I was told that when he was in high school, he was a swimmer, and half the girls in the stands showed up just to see him in his Speedo. Apparently, he had that kind of presence.

Much like Susan, he always seemed to need a companion. I never knew him to be without a girlfriend or a wife. It was as if he was uncomfortable being alone, too. It turns out that I was like both of my parents in that way.

Robert was nineteen years old when I was born. He grew up in the same small timber town as Susan. He was born, raised, worked, and died in that town. He never moved away and rarely left town, even for vacations or for any other reasons. Like Susan, college was not part of Robert's future. At fifteen, he worked alongside his brother at his dad's machine repair shop. Repairing and rebuilding heavy equipment, as well as occasionally someone's car or truck, ultimately became his career path. When his father passed away, Robert inherited the family business.

Along with his brother, Robert was raised by a rugged, alcoholic father and a loving, alcoholic mother. My paternal grandpa was an interesting man. Most people knew him around town because of his long-standing local business or his daily drinking habit at the neighborhood bar. He gave off this rough, take-no-shit-from-anyone vibe, yet I remember getting away with just about anything around him. He was kind to me but came across as obnoxious, rude, and stern to most people. Or at least that is how I perceived how others would see him.

When I visited his machine shop, he'd repeatedly tell me not to call him Grandpa in front of his customers. Of course, the minute a customer showed up, I'd call him Grandpa right away. He'd always act like I annoyed him, but I knew that wasn't true. I would often catch him cracking a smile as he walked away. Breaking through his grouchy old man exterior made me feel like I had very magical powers.

He had a pug named Jäger. The dog earned its name from drinking Jägermeister. My grandpa would take that dog to the bar across the street from his shop, put it on a barstool next to him, pull a saucer out of his pocket, and ask the bartender to pour a shot of Jägermeister for the dog. Ugh, that poor dog. Can you imagine seeing a dog sitting on a bar stool drinking? How that dog lived as long as it did is beyond me.

My grandpa was an interesting man, that's for sure. He passed away during my senior year of high school. It was the first time I experienced the death of someone I knew. I acknowledged his death with a great deal of indifference. I felt like I should feel grief and sadness, but I didn't. Maybe I just didn't let myself feel the loss after everything I'd already been through, or maybe somehow it just felt safer to shut down any emotion that hinted I might care about someone. I remember feeling numb. I didn't have the capability to process his death in any meaningful way.

According to my family, my grandmother—Robert's mom— was my constant companion during my infancy and toddler years. During that time in my life, Robert would drop me off at her house each day before going to work. Although I have no clear memories of those early days I spent with her, I can still sense the immense love she had for me. There's something powerful about the bonds formed in those early years, even when they escape our conscious memory. Most children don't begin forming lasting memories until around age three or four, and by the time I reached that age, Susan had already pulled me away from Robert and, by extension, from my grandmother, too.

I was able to reconnect with my grandmother while I was in high school and living with Susan's parents. She was kind but slightly distant towards me and quiet in a way that seemed more than just a personality trait. Compared to her husband and sons, who had loud, commanding presences, she almost faded into the background. Perhaps she had learned to make herself small, to stay out of the way—a survival strategy I knew all too well.

I often witnessed my grandfather speaking to her harshly, with a tone that left unseen emotional bruises. She carried herself with quiet strength, but I saw the wear on her body and in her eyes. Eventually, I came to understand why she found escape in a vodka bottle—she was seeking solace wherever and whenever she could.

Because they were all from the same small town and in the same high school class, Robert, Susan, and Chip—the man Susan married at seventeen—knew one another. From what I can piece together, I don't think Robert and Chip were as into drugs as Susan, but they all liked to drink. The school was small enough that they ran in the same circles, and in that era and at that age, I can only imagine all the "free love and sexual promiscuity."

Because Robert's family's machine repair shop was the only one in their rural community and because it also serviced all the vehicles for the local mill, Robert was granted a draft deferment. His job was deemed essential by the local draft board, so Robert was one of the few teenage boys left in town by the end of 1966.

He never talked with me about what it was like to see fifteen of his high school buddies get drafted when he stayed in town. I have a feeling he was relieved, but I wonder if he also felt like he missed out on some of the action. Chip and three other guys he knew never made it home. I'm sure that must have been devastating to experience.

Robert knew Susan was married to Chip when they hooked up. Maybe a combination of Susan's free-love vibe and Robert's charisma brought them together. Who knows. I can also see how both of them might have been hurting and needed to numb out with someone who was equally as emotionally unavailable. One thing I do know for sure is that Robert said they had a lot of sex on the couch in the office of my grandfather's shop. To this day, I have no idea why my dad felt compelled to share that information with me, but he did. And wouldn't you know it, that is the place where I was conceived.

According to Robert, Susan used to constantly say, "I can't have children." She claimed she was barren and made it clear that if she ever did become pregnant, she would have an abortion. He was perfectly fine with that; fatherhood had never been something he wanted. So when Susan unexpectedly became pregnant, Robert was genuinely shocked. But something clearly shifted in him because, once the reality of creating a child set in, he warmed to the idea. In fact, he was the one who convinced Susan not to go through with the abortion.

I never asked him what stirred that sense of responsibility enough to want to become my father.

During the first year of my life, Robert, Susan, and I lived in a small house just four doors down from his parents. I don't know why Robert and Susan divorced when I was just about a year old, but that decision set the course for what came next. After their separation, I stayed with Robert, which is how I came to spend so much time with his mother. Even now, it's unusual for a father to have sole custody of an infant, but in the late 1960s, such arrangements were virtually unheard of. At such a young age, I found his willingness to have sole custody of me impressive.

From what I have learned, it sounded like Susan slid back into her drug-loving ways, which meant she wasn't able to take care of me. Town gossip whispered that Susan was sleeping around after I was born, and maybe Robert and his family just didn't want to have anything more to do with her. I think it's possible he may have forced her into a divorce and demanded that she leave us.

Even though I don't have conscious memories from those early years of my life, I know that being left by my mother created a lasting imprint on my subconscious. As I've come to understand more about how personalities develop, I've learned that unstable or unpredictable environments can disrupt a child's ability to establish key self-regulatory skills—such as emotional control, impulse management, and the capacity to plan or cope. These are the very foundations we rely on to navigate the world. I don't doubt that Robert and his parents did their best to care for me, but still, some part of me must have longed for Susan, even if I couldn't yet form the words to say so.

I have almost no memory of living with Robert as an infant and toddler. Fortunately, we had that second chance when I moved in with Susan's parents. Ironically—or perhaps ideally—he had recently moved out of the house four doors down from his parents and into the one next door to Susan's parents. Only in a small town could such a twist of geography cause fate to unfold. That little shift in proximity—closer to Robert, farther from Susan—gave us the space and time to reconnect slowly and piece together our earlier bond.

When Susan's parents picked me up from the bus stop the day I arrived from Oregon, we pulled into the driveway of their weathered two-story house. As I looked at it for the first time, the only thought in my head was, *It's so small. How do they live here? How am I going to live here?* The green paint was chipped and faded, and the three wooden steps leading up to the porch sagged tiredly in the middle.

Slygore said, *This sucks. You're gonna hate living in this place.* Athena softly countered with, *You're a survivor. You'll find a way to fit in.*

As I emerged from the car, I saw a man sitting on the porch next door. He turned to watch us and waved hello.

"Who's that?" I asked.

My grandpa said, "That's your biological father."

I felt awful that I didn't even recognize him; admittedly, it was getting dark, and I hadn't seen him since I was a very little girl.

I realized, at the time, that living next door to him would either be a great thing or an absolutely horrible experience. My grandparents and I each took a suitcase and walked up the sagging front steps and into their house. Grandma showed me to my room upstairs, Susan's old room. The window looked over the quiet street, and although the house was weathered on the outside, it was well-kept on the inside. A vase of colorful flowers sat on a small desk, brightening my entire room.

"It's not much, but it's all yours," my grandmother said. "We didn't have much advance notice of your arrival. If you need anything else to help you feel comfortable, just let us know, honey. I know it has been a long day for you. So get settled in tonight, and we'll see you downstairs for breakfast tomorrow morning."

As I settled into my new bedroom, I couldn't remember the last breakfast with Susan and Roger. Probably never.

In the morning, smells of bacon and pancakes drifted up the stairs to my room. As the sun rose, I was glad that my bedroom window faced east, allowing me to see the bright sunlight streaming through my windows. I walked down the stairs and found Grandma and Grandpa sitting at the small square table, reading the newspaper with plates of steaming bacon, eggs, and pancakes in front of them. This seemed like something right out of the movies. The tasty smell of the buffet-like breakfast ensured that I was not dreaming.

"Good morning, Julie," my grandpa said.

"Good morning," I muttered.

Grandma chimed in, saying, "Help yourself to some of the food, honey. It's on the stovetop. I know you've just arrived, and I want to give you some time to get acquainted with the place, but you need to think about your summer plans. I heard the cafe down the street could use some help. I imagine you'd like to earn some spending money. Your grandpa and I can keep you housed and fed, and we have a bicycle for you so you can get around town, but we don't have much more to offer you other than that. We are retired and don't have much of an income." My grandpa kept reading the paper and nodded his head in agreement.

That was fine with me. I was just grateful to have a place to stay and grateful my grandparents took me in. Above all, I was glad everything seemed pretty normal. "Sounds good. Will you take me down there later to introduce me, or should I go alone?" I asked.

"I'll take you," My grandpa replied. "Now, eat before your food gets cold. You want part of the paper, sweetheart?"

And, just like that, I became part of a new—unexpectedly stable—household. That afternoon, I got a job bussing tables at The Sawmill Cafe. Luckily, the job was only part-time, leaving me plenty of time to explore my surroundings while making a little money and begin settling into my new life.

A few mornings later, I saw Robert, my dad, sitting on his back porch. With Athena whispering words of support in my ear and my own curiosity bubbling up inside, I found the courage to walk over and re-introduce myself.

"Hi, I'm Julie." After an awkward pause, I followed with, "You're my dad, right?" I remember thinking how ridiculous that sounded.

"I know, Julie. Would you like to sit down? Can I get you something to eat or drink? Your grandparents told me you were moving in."

Okay, here goes nothing, I thought. I sat down next to him awkwardly on the creaky steps. "You remember me?"

He looked at me with a small, sad smile and said, "Yes. Of course, I remember you, Julie. You're my daughter. How could I ever forget you?"

Silence hung for a moment between us, broken only by the sounds of chirping birds and rustling trees. I tried to remember to breathe, as Athena kept telling me to do.

Robert eventually continued, "I've missed you very much, Julie."

Well, that did it. My heart was racing, and my eyes started to well up. Though I didn't want it to, a single tear tracked down my cheek. We paused in silence, and then I bombarded him with questions, "Why haven't I seen you? Where have you been? Why did you let me go? Did I do something wrong?"

Robert looked at me with hurt and shame on his face. The look he gave me was flooded with a depth of emotion. "Yes, I wanted you in my life very badly. I want to tell you everything. Are you sure you want to hear it all?"

With more tears now streaming uncontrollably down my face, I somehow managed to squeak out the word, "Yes."

Robert sat in silence for a few moments, then began to speak. He told me about how Susan had taken me from him multiple times and deliberately prevented him from seeing me as I grew up. He told me he'd sent cards and gifts over the years, and I told him I'd never received them. As I listened to this man, who still felt more like a stranger than a father, recount how he'd been wronged and attempted to justify the choices that had shaped my life, I realized that I wasn't interested in the whole backstory.

I was in the middle of trying to sort out my own pain and confusion. I didn't have the space to process his regrets and excuses. Yet, beneath the bitterness in his voice and lingering resentment toward Susan, I heard numerous traces of grief and heartache. It was clear that some part of him wished things had turned out differently.

He seemed desperate to tell me his side of everything, seemingly in defense of whatever action or inaction he had once chosen to take. He talked. I listened and kept trying not to tune him out. As he rambled on and on, my mind drifted off a few times. None of what he was describing really mattered anymore, at least not to me. The past couldn't be undone. And then, like a jolt to get my meandering mind back on track, he asked, "How do you feel about all of this, Julie?"

Wait, what? I thought, stunned. No one had ever asked me how I felt about any of it. I didn't know how to respond. I just stared at him in disbelief. A flicker of hurt crossed my face. After a pause, I mumbled, "Okay, I guess. It's fine. I'm not mad at you." I quickly looked away.

I dodged the question, not because I didn't have any feelings, but because I had too many feelings. They were all jumbled and overwhelming. Saying them aloud would've meant admitting, to both Robert and myself, that I was confused, hurt, angry, and deeply sad. And in that moment, I didn't have the heart to hurt him any further. So I just sat there, drying my eyes and holding in my emotions—it seemed like the best way to keep the peace.

I questioned if he really cared about how I felt because he didn't challenge my reply, but in truth, he was probably just as uncomfortable as I was, which would've explained why he just took me at my word. Slygore whispered, *He's just being polite. He's not interested in your feelings. He doesn't give a shit about you, and you know it.*

In response, I silently told Slygore, *Shut up and leave me alone.* Here was a man, my own biological dad, desperately trying to reconnect with me and make up for lost time. Even though I was angry at him, why in the world would I tell him how I really felt? It just seemed cruel.

I told myself, *What happened in the past was no big deal. Robert seems to genuinely like you, Julie, and Susan hates you right now, so don't fuck this relationship up too. Just shut up and move forward.* So, I did just that. Suppression was my silent strategy. I needed to keep Robert happy. I needed him to like me.

The only way I could think of to deal with my unwanted and uncomfortable emotions was to escape the moment. I said, "It's been nice talking with you, but I've got to go now. I look forward to spending time with you and getting to know you better." My polite veneer was ever-present. I knew how to wear that fake smile well.

It wasn't until months later, after we'd gotten to know each other better, that the mask I had become accustomed to wearing with him slowly started peeling away. I learned that I could be myself with Robert, but I never did tell him how I honestly felt that day we talked on his porch.

During my high school years, I lived with Susan's parents, but Robert, his girlfriend Lauren, and Robert's side of the family authentically started showing up for me. They looked out for me, invited me in, and carved out space for me in their lives. Little by little, I got to know my paternal grandparents, my aunt and uncles, and even my great-uncles. It felt incredible to have a new connection to family, but it also felt like they were frantically yet quietly making up for lost time.

Anytime the swirl of emotion became overwhelming for me, Athena would appear in my mind, her voice a soothing balm, saying, *Don't worry. This is all new. It will be okay. Just breathe. You'll be okay.*

But Slygore, the ever-present shadow, would counter with a cold whisper, *None of these people would've reached out if Susan hadn't kicked you out. No one fought for you when you were a child. They didn't want you then. They don't want you now. They're just being nice. Wake up, Julie. Don't be so stupid!* He was always good at reminding me not to trust people.

Despite Slygore's warnings, I began to open up and allow myself to be seen. I softened and permitted myself to be loved—to a degree. I found I genuinely enjoyed being part of a family, at least most of the time. My life also felt surreal, as if I had stepped into someone else's story, but there were moments when I truly felt like I belonged.

Those years brought a sense of grounding I hadn't known before. I felt accepted by Robert's family, as though I had a place in the world. The only time I felt out of sync was during family gatherings where alcohol flowed freely. As the volume rose and people got loud and rowdy, I'd shrink, look for the nearest exit, and make my way back to my grandparents' house.

In those moments, I was particularly thankful for Susan's parents. They didn't drink, and their home always remained steady, quiet, and easy. No matter what chaos unfolded outside, I always knew I could find peace there. It was the one safe space for me in the world.

Remember I said that Robert had a way with the ladies back in his younger days? Well, in my sophomore year of high school—in fact, during the very first week of me being the new kid at school yet again—a girl named Janet threw me for a huge loop.

The girl who approached me had permed brown hair, oversized hoop earrings, a skin-tight bright red tee-shirt under a jean jacket, and her jeans seemed intentionally ripped at the knees. "Hi, I'm Janet; I'm a senior. You're new here, right?"

"Yep, I'm Julie," I said.

"I know. Everyone knows who you are. You're Robert's kid. You don't look like him, you know."

"You know Robert?"

"Sure. All the girls in town know Robert. Even though he's an old guy, he's still the sexiest man in town. I love watching him working in his shop. His ass looks so good when he's bent over a big piece of equipment, if ya know what I mean."

"No, I don't know what you mean." I snapped, confusion and disgust played across my face. Her comment was so weird. I was uncomfortable talking to this girl about my dad, especially like that. Robert was in his mid-thirties, and Janet couldn't have been more than eighteen.

"I go by the shop all the time to talk to the young guys. Although girls don't usually like to work on big machinery, I'm pretty good at it. Robert has been great about showing me a few things. I sometimes get all tingly standing beside him, especially when he has his hands on mine, showing me how to tighten all the bolts. Last week, at the end of the day, we sat out back and had a few beers together."

"Huh. Okay." Athena whispered to me, *Politely walk away now. This girl is trouble.* "I'll see you around. I've gotta go." I told her.

"Oh, before you go, there's one more thing. Robert's my dad, too."

What? Is this girl insane? She's just playing with me, I thought. "I'm sorry, what did you say?"

"Robert's my dad, too. That's what makes it so fun to hang out with him. He has absolutely no idea, and honestly, I think he has the hots for me, too. He's screwed almost every woman in town. So why not me?"

I stared at her, and my jaw clenched. I had a pit in my stomach. I could barely find the words but managed to say, "Right, okay, ya weirdo." Then I turned and walked away.

She called after me, "My mom's name is Sharon. Ask Robert. She used to watch him in school when he was on the swim team. See ya 'round, sis." Then, she jogged down the hall to catch up with some of her friends. It was one of the oddest encounters I've ever had in my life.

That afternoon, I rode my bike over to the machine repair shop. I walked into the loud, cavernous, open space with concrete floors. A beat-up old forklift was on one of the lifts, and a massive green plowing tractor was taking up half of the work area. Tools were neatly organized in boxes, and a few were scattered on the workbench at the back of the shop. The unforgettable metallic scent of oil and grease filled my nose, along with a subtle undercurrent of solvent. I said hi to one of the shop guys, hugged my grandfather, and walked over to Robert, who had his torso slung into the engine compartment of the tractor. I tried hard not to look at his ass and failed because Janet's ridiculous words were stuck in my brain.

The noise in the shop at that moment was deafening, so I shouted, "Hey, Robert, do you have a minute to talk?"

"Sure, just let me finish tightening this bolt. I'm almost done for the day anyway. Why don't we go out back and sit in the sunshine?" He finished what he was doing, stood up from his hunched position, and put down his wrench. We walked out the shop's back door and settled into a couple of sun-beaten canvas lawn chairs. "What's up?" he said.

I told him I had met a girl named Janet, who was a senior at school. I then mentioned that she is the girl who likes to hang out here at the shop sometimes.

"Oh, Janet. Sure. I know her. She's pretty good with tools and a quick learner. I think she likes the attention from the guys a little too much, but she seems like a good enough kid."

"Um . . . She told me she is your daughter," I said awkwardly.

Robert's face shifted and turned quizzical. He paused for what felt like minutes, then said, "Huh. That's news to me. Do you know Janet's mom's name?"

"She said it was Sharon. She said Sharon liked to watch you swim when you were on the swim team in high school."

He paused again, half smiled, then said, "Yeah, that's possible. Janet could be my kid. Is that why she hangs around here?"

I felt my body flinch, and a wave of confusion came over me. Silence descended as my heart tightened. I stared at him. All I could say was, "Do I have other half-siblings?"

With a heavy sigh, he replied, "Honestly, I don't know, kid. I certainly won't ever claim them if I find out about them." He told me, almost casually, that with so many young men sent off to Vietnam, someone had to stay behind and "keep the girls happy." It was a crude confession, delivered with a shrug as if it were just part of the times, and maybe it was. He went on to admit that, in the back of his mind, he often wondered if some of the other babies born around town might be his—but he never asked. Nor would he. He didn't want the responsibility, especially if it meant paying child support.

To this day, I don't know if I have more than one half-sibling. But I do believe I have at least one half-sister. Whether or not Robert and Sharon ever proved that Janet was the result of their brief romance is unclear, but the possibility certainly exists.

Because we were two grades apart, I never spent much time with Janet. She wasn't exactly the type of person I wanted to be around. We didn't hang in the same circles, and we certainly didn't feel like sisters—especially since I knew she had a "crush," or whatever she called it, on Robert while knowing he might be her dad. The entire situation was too weird for me. After she graduated, Janet moved away, and I never saw her again.

Robert was raised in a home where drinking wasn't just normalized—it was practically ritualized. I remember him once saying that his mother used Frangelico in pancake batter when he was a kid. In their household, alcohol was as ordinary as butter or salt, and that's not an exaggeration.

I share this because of its influence—not just on Robert, but on me and the relationship we tried to rebuild. The paternal side of my family has long been marked by drinking problems, and that history has profoundly shaped the way I've moved through the world. It's one of the main reasons I've kept my distance from that side of the family for much of my adult life. I've always been finely attuned to unpredictability, and over the years, I learned that people who drank or used drugs excessively were often the most emotionally volatile. Being around that kind of chaos never felt safe.

It's not easy to admit, but for a long time, I struggled to accept other people's choices when they didn't align with my own definitions of right and wrong, good and bad. That black-and-white kind of thinking is something I'm actively working to shift because it no longer serves me.

Losing a parent has a way of stirring something deep, forcing you to face your own mortality. Robert's death was no exception. His passing opened a doorway into compassion, forgiveness, and a more nuanced understanding of who we both were.

In his later years, I made the conscious decision to create distance between us, not out of anger, but from the painful reality of his alcohol addiction. It became too difficult for me to watch him slowly unravel, to witness the toll his drinking was taking on both his body and his mind. From time to time, I checked in with his wife, mostly to see how his health was holding up. But the truth is, my ego couldn't handle the choices he was making.

Back then, I still carried the illusion that I could control others, believing that if people loved me, they would change for me. When he didn't, I stepped away. I chose not to be fully present in his life.

After he passed away, I began to recognize how I abandoned him in the last few years of his life. It's difficult to admit, but it's true. And the irony isn't lost on me. For so long, I held onto the pain of being the one who was left behind—the one who Robert and Susan both discarded. However, with time and perspective, I can see my own choices through a much wider lens. And maybe, just maybe, I'm beginning to understand Robert's choices, too.

I sometimes wonder if, when Susan took me away from him, Robert's ego told him he couldn't win? That fighting for me wasn't worth facing off with Susan and the weight of Stan's money and influence? Did he convince himself it was easier to let me go than step into that battle? I'll never really know, but I can see how fear, pride, and helplessness can masquerade as indifference. It's interesting to consider that Robert left before I could remember him, but he came back hoping to repair what time and silence had frayed. I wanted to let him in, and for a while, I did. But near the end, I was the one who pulled away. Maybe that's what shadows do—they come and go, until we finally learn to face them.

Robert passed away at the age of seventy. After working in a machine repair shop his entire life and not wearing any protective equipment to reduce exposure to chemical fumes, dust, and asbestos, he developed lung cancer. Several years before his death, the cancer became nearly debilitating. I can't imagine what it must have been like to have every breath feel like a chore.

Eventually, depression set in for Robert, which ramped up his alcoholism, and he began to rely on liquor instead of food for nourishment. His body finally gave way, and so did his will to live.

As I shifted out of my reminiscence, I handed Laura a framed image, "Here is a photo of us, taken while we lived next door to each other."

"Wow, what a great photo. Your dad is indeed pretty handsome. You lucked out with your gene pool, Julie," Laura said with a massive grin on her face as she stared at the image for a few seconds. "Losing a parent is unlike any other loss. I lost my mom a few years ago. The permanence of this kind of loss has a unique impact on one's life, that's for sure. It's like losing a part of yourself." Laura returned the photo to me.

I nodded and replied, "That's exactly what it felt like, Laura—like losing a part of myself. When Robert passed away, his death touched me more deeply than I ever expected. We never had a traditional father-daughter bond, nor were we especially close. But still, something within me stirred. His leaving this world created an unexpected ache, a quiet sorrow I hadn't anticipated. Hmmm, maybe neither of us ever really walked away from one another—we simply loved one another in the best way we knew how."

FIVE

Lily began to wiggle and squirm, which indicated to me that she needed another potty break and her daily walk. The drizzle that had come in after lunch had now passed, and I was delighted to see patches of blue sky amid high clouds. I had been so engrossed in the details of Robert's life that I'd barely noticed the change in weather.

"Laura, would you be up for a walk with Lily and me? There's a lovely paved trail that wanders the neighborhood and even hugs the coastline. I can tell you about my other dad, Stan, as we walk and enjoy some nice sunshine."

"Oh, I'd love that," Laura exclaimed. "My hips are getting a bit sore after sitting for so long." Laura rose from the leather chair and winced a little as she stood up. "I'm not as young as I used to be," Laura added and leaned over to switch off her recorder. "I'll need to go and get my sneakers out of my car."

"Sounds good, Laura. You can use the side entrance; it's closer to the driveway. I'll get my shoes on and Lily harnessed up while you're getting your sneakers.

I looked at Lily and said, "Who's ready for a walk? Are you ready for a walk?" With her thick chocolate tail wagging with excitement, Lily began scampering to the exterior side door that was just beyond the large mud room.

Laura set her seemingly bottomless tote bag on the built-in bench and headed out to her car. I laced up my sneakers, grabbed a light windbreaker, and put Lily in her bright green and pink camo harness. We met Laura outside, and the three of us headed down the long driveway to the side street.

As we neared the trail entrance—about an eighth of a mile down the quiet road—Laura opened her recording app and handed me a small device. She said, "If you slip this into your chest pocket, it will pick up what you're saying just fine." I slipped the microphone into my pocket, and we headed out for a five-mile scenic walk.

Lily, with her tongue already hanging from the side of her mouth, led the way, and with a twinge of eagerness, I began to tell Laura about Stan.

According to my Aunt Georgia, Stan was smitten with me from the very first moment we met. And honestly, I can see why; I was a pretty adorable little kid.

Stan was in his mid-thirties with no biological children of his own, meeting this chubby, pigtailed, blonde-haired ball of energy for the first time. I was silly, talkative, and wide-eyed— the kind of child who knew how to command a room and was always hungry for attention. He may have fallen in love with Susan, but I like to think I was the one who sealed the deal.

Stan married Susan when I was just two years old, and though we weren't together full-time during every stage of my childhood, he became the single most steady and unwavering presence in my life. The few court documents I have paint a picture of an adoption process that was anything but easy for him. It took time, persistence, and an unwavering sense of commitment. Plenty of obstacles popped up, and he could have walked away at any point. No one would have blamed him.

Raising me required financial resources—money Stan could've spent elsewhere, on himself, or his future. But more than that, it required emotional presence, patience, and a lot of love. He could have directed those energies toward a career, a simpler life, or some other relationship. Instead, he chose me.

Stan had no obligation to adopt me when he married Susan. And yet, not only did he step into the role of a father, but he's never once stepped out of it. Stan has never abandoned me—not in presence, spirit, or love. We still talk regularly and try to see each other at least twice a year. I know, without a doubt, that I wouldn't be the person I am today without his steadfast influence.

To say I'm grateful doesn't even begin to cover it, Laura. What I feel for Stan is something deeper—a profound appreciation rooted in the kind of love that is chosen, nurtured, and never withheld.

In 1970, Stan was thirty-six, divorced, living in Denver, and building a quiet life for himself. He was handsome in a modest, unassuming way, with a medium build and a full head of thick, black curls. By day, he worked as a copier salesman, a practical job that suited his dependable nature. Although he is naturally introverted, Stan carries a calm steadiness that makes people feel safe around him. He is loving, loyal, and grounded—the kind of man who shows up without fanfare and follows through without needing any applause.

Even back then, he embodied the essence of a responsible and reliable family man. In many ways, he was, and still is, the classic all-American guy—predictable in the best sense of the word. And maybe that's exactly why he was drawn to Susan.

She was anything but typical, especially in her twenties. Where he was rooted, she was wild. Where he offered structure, she embodied freedom. Opposites often collide before they connect—and perhaps, in her unpredictability, Stan saw something exciting. Or maybe he simply saw someone who needed to be chosen.

Susan was twenty-two years old and worked as a cocktail waitress at a neighborhood tavern in Cherry Creek, near downtown Denver. How she ended up in Denver after leaving Robert is still a mystery to me. Maybe it was simply the nearest big city to the small Montana town where she'd grown up—a place far enough to start over yet familiar enough not to feel completely lost.

She and Stan met through a mutual friend, but the real story started before the friend even arrived. Stan walked into the tavern, scanning the room, when his eyes landed on Susan. In his version of the tale, it was as if a beam of light from heaven singled her out. She stood there—alive, radiant, magnetic—and something in him just knew. He sensed, in that instant, that she was no ordinary woman. She was electric. Untamed. The kind of person who could flip his world upside down and show him parts of life he would never have dared explore.

You know the old saying, opposites attract? Well, that was Stan and Susan. He was steady; she was wild. He built foundations; she chased the wind. And somehow, in that chaotic chemistry, they found a spark worth pursuing.

The Susan I knew was always looking for a man to take care of her, so she may have seen Stan as a stable provider for her and me. After dating for a couple of months, Susan finally told Stan that she had a two-year-old daughter who lived with her biological father in Montana. She knew that information would likely make or break the relationship, and she hoped he'd be open to having a daughter in his life.

Stan told me later that Susan had fed him a story about how awful Robert's parents were to her and that she felt the only way ever to find peace was to leave that small town. She knew Robert and his parents would look after me until she got settled somewhere new. She didn't tell him that the Montana court system had officially awarded Robert sole custody. No matter what she told him, she clearly knew how to spin the story because it pacified Stan enough that he wanted to stick around.

Stan came from a large family with five siblings, and he grew up with one older brother and three sisters. We never really talked much about his childhood. If I asked Stan specific questions, he would generally respond with a seemingly ordinary story about his family, his school, or his younger days. He never mentioned his dad, and what little I recall of his mom is that she was a kind and loving woman. Stan grew up in Wyoming, but after attending the University of Denver, he fell in love with the area so much that he decided to make Denver his home.

Because of Stan's large family, holiday gatherings, especially at Christmas and Thanksgiving, were a whirlwind of energy. The house overflowed with people, and laughter echoed through every room; the scent of home-cooked food drifted from the kitchen. Kids darted underfoot like sparks. It was both exhilarating and overwhelming for me—a sensory overload of voices, movement, and affection. The sheer volume of it all sometimes made me want to retreat to a quiet corner, but at the same time, I felt the electric hum of belonging. It was chaotic, yes, but it was also alive and, in its own way, fun and beautiful.

I remember the first holiday I spent with Stan's family. It was Thanksgiving, and it felt like I had stepped into another world. I was seated at what seemed like the world's longest kids' table, surrounded by cousins and second cousins whose names I hadn't yet learned. I sat there, slightly stunned, wide-eyed, and unsure, wanting to shrink into myself. I didn't know most of these people, and the sheer chaos of voices and activity left me feeling curious and also entirely out of place.

My cousins were boisterous and full of energy. They pulled me into their games and inside jokes, teasing me gently until they realized I responded better to warmth than to playful jabs. I imagine, to them, I was just the quiet, small-town little girl Uncle Stan had brought along—the new addition with big eyes and a tentative smile.

Susan, on the other hand, was unforgettable. She swept into the room in a floor-length, emerald-green velvet dress that clung to her curves and dipped daringly at the neckline. She shimmered with confidence, all energy and presence, and I'm pretty sure every man—and even the teenage boys—watched her with slack-jawed awe.

The kids' table sat adjacent to the even longer adult table, where no fewer than fifty people were gathered. Dishes passed from every direction, and the air was thick with the mouthwatering scent of roasted meats, warm bread, and sweet pies. Voices created a chaotic background of chatter, and the room buzzed with energy. It was loud, alive, and utterly foreign to me.

As an only child who often played four-person board games by herself—and yes, that was as sad as it sounds—the whole experience was disorienting but also fascinating. I looked around, trying to imagine what it must have been like to grow up like this, to always have someone nearby to talk to, laugh with, scheme with, or lean on. For Stan, this was normal. For me, it was a kind of magic I'd never known.

Two months later, Aunt Georgia hosted the Christmas gathering. She had a huge house, and in her living room stood a nearly two-story Christmas tree, which was perfectly decorated with twinkling lights and ornaments. I remember being fascinated with the massiveness of that tree.

Though Susan, Stan, and I had our own celebration at home, each of my cousins and I received one gift from under Aunt Georgia's tree. That year, I received a LEGO castle set, and I could hardly wait to take it home and start building. Even before we left her house, my mind was already spinning tales of fairy princesses and fearless knights. I remember thinking that it almost felt like Susan and Stan belonged to the world my imagination was creating.

After the flurry of gift-opening had settled and wrapping paper lay crumpled like snowdrifts across the floor, we gathered around the long tables for Christmas dinner. The smell of roasted ham and buttery mashed potatoes filled the air, mingling with the warmth of clinking glasses and various conversations.

About mid-way through dinner, at the adults' table, a slight commotion caught my eye. Stan's brother and Aunt Pam's husband were engaged in a petty tug-of-war—disagreeing, half-joking but serious, about who would get the coveted seat next to Susan, who on that day wore a form-flattering ruby red dress. Their voices rose just enough to draw attention, which sounded playful on the surface but was edged with a competitiveness that made nearly everyone glance over.

Stan, seated a few chairs down, simply shook his head, offering the trio a flat, unreadable look. Not annoyance. Not amusement. Just that quiet indifference he seemed to wear like armor—an expression that said, *This again?* He didn't intervene. He didn't need to. Susan's presence always created a ripple which Stan had already learned how to ride out.

After all the delicious food had made its rounds—passed up and down the tables, heaped onto plates, and eagerly devoured by every hungry mouth in the room—the post-feast lull began to settle in. Laughter softened to murmurs, forks clinked against nearly empty dishes, and people leaned back in their chairs with full stomachs and contented sighs.

Wanting to be helpful, I quietly began gathering the empty plates from the tables. I stacked my plate with a couple of the plates around me and trailed after Aunt Pam into the kitchen. She met up with Aunt Georgia, and as I put the plates on the counter with the other dirty dishes, my ear caught the low murmur of their voices. Pam and Georgia stood at the counter, their backs to me and their heads bent close. I hid behind the kitchen island to listen.

Aunt Georgia whispered, "Pam, did you see Susan in that dress? It's clear she's not wearing a bra. She's probably not even wearing underwear. I heard she spent her teen years hanging out with a hippie crowd."

Pam responded in a hushed hiss, "Of course I noticed! Whose husband do you think ended up sitting next to her? I swear, all the men here are drooling over her, and it seems like she's doing her very best to entice them. I don't know how Stan puts up with it or why he even married her in the first place!

She's not going to stick around with him forever. She's too wild for him."

"It's not our place to say," Georgia replied, though her tone suggested otherwise. "But the dresses she wears and how she acts around other men make me think she has an eye for someone more than Stan. I think she just married Stan for his money, even though he doesn't have much—or maybe it's for his stability; he definitely offers that. I really don't want her hanging around our family other than for big gatherings like these."

"I agree. I feel bad for keeping my kids away from Julie, but she might grow up to be just like her mother. I don't want her near my boys."

I was too young to fully grasp what they were saying, but I could feel the tension curling through the air like thick smoke. Their voices were sharp and laced with bitterness.

Georgia said, "It's not like Stan's blind. He knows what people are saying. He just wants to bury his head in the sand and think she'll stay true to him."

As they continued to rinse the dishes and put them in the dishwasher, it was clear they had no idea I was in the kitchen with them. Pam said, "Remember that first wife of Stan's? Same thing. Her beauty blinded him. We know how well that worked out."

At that moment, Susan entered the kitchen with a wine glass in each hand. My aunts fell silent. Susan had a bright, brittle smile plastered on her face. "Have you seen the wine? Your brother and I are looking for a refill."

Georgia and Pam exchanged a quick, almost imperceptible glance. "The wine is over there in the pantry," said Georgia, pointing with a wooden spoon.

Susan's smile flickered—just for a second—then tightened into something harder, more practiced. Without a word, she turned toward the pantry, her dress swishing around her like a whisper. I watched her leave the room, thinking how beautiful she looked, even as something in the air shifted.

As soon as she disappeared from view, Aunt Pam leaned toward Georgia and hissed, "Poor Stan. I bet the only good thing to come out of his marriage to Susan is having Julie be his little girl."

I froze for a moment, unsure what to do, then quietly backed out of the kitchen, careful not to make a sound. Neither of them ever knew I'd heard a word of their conversation.

At the time, I didn't understand what they meant by "poor Stan." He seemed perfectly fine to me. He drove a nice car, we had plenty of money, and he bought me quite a few Strawberry Shortcake dolls—clear signs of a good life in my young eyes. But something in their tone, the sharpness behind the sweetness, kept gnawing at me.

Even then, I sensed it. Some people, some truths, carried a shadow. At that moment, I understood on a level too deep for language that the shadow had something to do with Susan. She was, in their eyes, a kind of trouble. Not loud. Not obvious. But a hushed kind of trouble—the slow, simmering kind.

Slygore kept me company in the back seat of the car as Stan, Susan, and I drove home from the party. *Your mother is trouble. Nobody loves you. Everybody hates you. You suck, and you should go eat worms.* That last line was always Slygore's favorite.

My cousins lived nearby, but as Georgia and Pam had promised, we only saw Stan's family during the big holidays— Thanksgiving, Christmas, and at the giant family picnic once each summer. What I heard in that kitchen that Christmas stayed buried inside me for years, like a secret I didn't quite know I was keeping. It wasn't until much later that I consciously realized that most of Stan's family didn't dislike Susan outright—they were just uneasy around her. Her free spirit and unconventional way of being unsettled something in them.

And maybe, even back then, it started to unsettle something in me, too.

While I was growing up, Stan stuck to his career as a copier salesman. As a kid, I remember thinking his job had to be the most boring one in the world—going from office to office trying to convince people to buy copy machines. It sounded dull and unimaginative. But Stan loved it. He believed in what he did, and more importantly, he let me into his world.

He was often on the road, crisscrossing the region in his immaculate company car. It seemed like he'd get a new one every couple of years, and they were always modest and practical. I once asked why he didn't get a sports car like the ones in the commercials, and he chuckled. "Copier salesmen aren't supposed to be flashy," he said. "And besides, sports cars aren't nearly as comfortable when you spend six hours a day behind the wheel."

Before each of his trips, we'd sit together on the living room floor with a pile of those old AAA maps spread out between us like a treasure hunt. He'd name the cities and towns where he had appointments—Cheyenne, Pueblo, Grand Junction—and ask me to help him find them. At first, I was clueless, overwhelmed by the maze of lines and symbols. But Stan patiently showed me how to use the legend, how to flip to the city index on the back, and how to trace my finger across the paper to find the shortest or most scenic route.

I'd study the map like it held some great secret, and I'd be proud when I found the right road before he did. It became our little ritual, making his work feel less like a job and more like a shared adventure. He used to say living in Denver was perfect for a traveling salesman because he was within driving distance of just about anywhere worth going.

Looking back, those moments weren't really about the maps or the miles. They were about connection, about him letting me be part of something that mattered to him. I like to think he was showing me that the journey, any journey, is more meaningful when you don't take it alone.

Sometimes, Stan would even bring out his briefcase, battered from years of use, and announce with excitement, "Alright, Julie, it's time to practice my sales pitch. You get to be the office manager at a big law firm, and I'll try to sell you the latest Xerox 914 copier."

He'd open the catalog and flip to the glossy photo of the machine, holding it out with the same reverence some men reserved for classic cars. My eyes would bounce between the picture and his practiced salesman's smile.

"This model," he'd say, brimming with enthusiasm, "is the future of office efficiency! It does it all. Of course, it copies faster and clearer than anything you've ever seen, but it also collates, staples, and folds, and even can make a cup of coffee." Stan would say with a shrug of his shoulders and a massive grin on his face. "I'm kidding about the coffee, of course. But, imagine Ms. Julie, no more tedious manual labor. Time is money, and this machine saves both. It's revolutionary!"

Caught up in his energy, I'd clap my hands like an eager customer, encouraging him to keep going.

He would chuckle and lean in towards me. "Now, here's the most important thing, Ms. Julie. We know your law office is booming—papers flying everywhere, deadlines all around. You don't have time for paper jams, blurry prints, or endless waiting, do you? That's where the Xerox 914 comes in. It's not just a copier. It's a solution. It's peace of mind."

Then, with a dramatic pause and a twinkle in his eye, he'd ask, "Now, Ms. Julie, as the office manager, what's your biggest problem?"

I'd furrow my brow, playing along, pretending to ponder deeply before replying, "Hmm . . . probably keeping track of everything, Stan. Like knowing which copies go together and who they're for. It's not an easy task."

"Exactly!" he'd say with a proud grin. Then came the close. The practiced finale always made me giggle. "And what if I told you this copier could solve that problem? With the Xerox 914, you're not just buying a copier; you're investing in the future of your business. You're investing in efficiency, productivity, and peace of mind. And at this price, you can't afford to say no!"

I'd laugh and say, "I think you're gonna sell a lot of copiers, sir!"

These little rituals—the map sessions on the living room floor and pretend sales calls with me as the client—helped ease the ache of his time away. They made me feel seen and included, as if I were part of something important. But the truth was that when Stan left for his business trips, I still missed him deeply.

Stan's job often took him away for a week or two at a time, long enough that his absence became woven into the rhythm of my childhood. He worked hard to support us, and he showed up in his own quiet, dependable ways. But what I remember most often about my childhood years with him was that he was absent—a lot.

When Stan was on the road, it was just Susan and me in the house, and those stretches felt endless. She spent most of her time on the phone, chain-smoking, or getting buzzed while reading trashy romance novels. Our home just didn't feel quite as safe or warm when he was gone.

I remember wondering to myself, *Why does he have to have that job? Can't he have a normal dad job where he comes home every night like other kids' dads?*

One of the best parts of Stan's trips was the gifts he'd often bring home. You could probably call them guilt gifts, but as a kid, I didn't really care about the meaning behind them. Here's a fun side note . . . I recall learning about the idiom of "not looking a gift horse in the mouth" in fourth grade. Our teacher, Miss MacInernay, told us that the idiom came from checking a horse's mouth and teeth to assess its age, value, and health. In ancient times, it would have been considered extremely rude to evaluate the horse carefully if it was given as a gift. At least, that's how I remember her telling us the story. Whenever Stan handed me a present, I smiled extra wide and kept any questions to myself. So, in essence, I was unknowingly practicing gratitude even at that young age.

My favorite gifts were the fake Strawberry Shortcake dolls. They didn't have the sweet strawberry smell like the real ones, but I didn't really care. I probably had more knock-off dolls than I had pairs of underwear at that point, and I was thrilled about that. Stan always told me that "he knew a guy who knew a guy," which was how he was able to buy so many fake ones. When he'd tell me that, I would picture Stan in some back alleyway wheeling and dealing for black market Strawberry Shortcake dolls. He was like the ultimate superhero negotiator to me. It's been a long time since I've thought about the endless amount of dolls Stan bought me. It's funny the things we remember.

After each trip, Stan would tell me stories about his time on the road—silly clients, dinners at fancy restaurants, late nights entertaining. Sometimes, he'd complain about the pressure to stay out and entertain clients who'd take offense if he called it a night too early. He'd say it was rough, but I think he secretly enjoyed that part of his job.

I'm not sure how Susan ever got used to Stan being gone so often—maybe she never really did. And neither did I. Between Stan and Robert, I spent much of my early life as a fatherless daughter. One gone by necessity, the other by choice. Their absence left an empty sort of space inside me—something quiet, unfinished, and hard to name.

I carried the feeling of abandonment from both paternal figures—emotionally, physically, and energetically. It wasn't until much later, just a few years ago, that I truly understood the depth of influence a father has on a daughter. This relationship affects her sense of self-worth, confidence, creativity, authority, and relationships. Looking back, I see how the absence of a consistent, present father figure played into the patterns that haunted me in adulthood. I struggled to form secure, lasting relationships. I clung too tightly, fearing loss, and then pushed people away the moment I felt vulnerable. I wanted love desperately, but once I had it, I often sabotaged it—because I never quite believed it would stay.

Perhaps that's why Susan eventually asked Stan for the separation and divorce the first time and moved us to San Francisco. After he took us back, Susan gave him an ultimatum. He needed to find a job that didn't require travel, or she'd leave again.

Stan, responsible and reliable by nature, found himself caught in an impossible bind. He was torn between providing for his family and the desire to keep the family together. It was the classic paradox; the very thing he did to support us was the same thing that threatened to pull us apart.

The decision to leave the career he had poured himself into for years must have been mentally and financially devastating. He never talked about the toll it took, and I was too young to ask. I didn't realize until much later that we were no longer living off a paycheck but off the quiet reserves of his savings. He had given up the security of his livelihood to try and save his marriage and his family.

Several months had passed, and Stan still hadn't found a new sales job that would keep him local. What began as a plea for him to be home more often had now morphed into something else entirely. Susan was no longer relieved by his presence; she was furious about it. The very thing she once demanded now seemed to irritate her to no end.

It was like watching someone wrestle with their own self-reflection. One day, she longed for stability; the next, she recoiled from it like it was a trap. She couldn't seem to decide what she wanted—from Stan, from her marriage, or from herself. Stan was left trying to read the shifting tides of her moods and navigating a minefield of unrealistic expectations that seemed to change by the hour.

I could relate to his dilemma all too well.

One night, I was supposed to be asleep, but I crept out of bed to get a drink of water. The house was still and dark. It was the kind of quiet that felt too heavy to be peaceful. I heard their low yet tense voices as I passed the living room.

I peeked around the corner and saw Susan sitting rigidly at one end of the couch with her arms crossed. Her voice cut through the silence. "This is ridiculous, Stan. When are you going back to work? You need to make money. We can't live on air or off the crumbs of your savings. You promised to take care of me. And Julie, too."

Stan sat slouched at the couch's other end, looking small in a way I'd never seen before, almost defeated. He said, "I'm trying, Susan. Really, I'm trying. You know I am. I've put in applications everywhere."

"Trying doesn't pay the bills, Stan," she snapped. "I'm not going to sit here and watch you mope around like some washed-up has-been."

"I gave up my job for you," Stan said finally, his tone laced with bitterness. "You told me you couldn't handle me being gone all the time. So I quit my job. And now that I'm around more, it's like you can't wait for me to disappear."

"Yes, I wanted you home, but not unemployed and sulking around like a lost child. How hard can it be to get a job, Stan? Get off your fucking ass and provide for your family. Because if you don't, I swear I'm gone. And this time, I won't be back. If I have to go back to work, I'm not sharing a damn cent with you."

My stomach twisted. I forgot about being thirsty and quietly slipped back to bed, holding my breath like it might keep the walls from collapsing around me. I pulled the blanket over my head and tried to push their conversation out of my mind, but I couldn't. I knew Susan was serious, and I began preparing for the worst.

And just like that, Susan filed for divorce two months later—again. She packed up our lives and moved us to Durango, leaving Stan behind, alone in the ruins of everything he'd sacrificed to keep us together.

Living life like that as a kid kept my head spinning and my emotions buried.

Even though Stan and Susan's marriage didn't survive, Stan has always remained in my life in one way or another. A few days after I landed at my grandparents' house in Montana, after Susan kicked me out, Stan showed up.

I couldn't believe it. He came for me. I was elated. I liked my grandparents well enough, and I was curious about my new relationship with Robert, but Stan . . . Stan was my dad. And when he arrived, I just knew he was there to take me home with him.

After greeting my grandparents with quiet politeness, he turned to me and said softly, "Come on, kiddo. Let's go for a walk."

The late afternoon golden sun slanted low in the sky, casting long shadows across his face. To me, he looked older. More tired and worn. The man with the sparkling eyes who made adventures from maps and copier pitches had dulled. But his voice was calming, grounded, and gentle.

"Julie, I know this isn't how we pictured things turning out. It's certainly not what I wanted, and I know you didn't either. I have no idea what is going on with your mom, and I'm sorry she sent you away."

I stared at him numbly. Susan's words, sharp and final, echoed cruelly in my mind: *I don't want to see you again—ever.*

With his head lowered, he said, "Your mom has made her choice about you being at the ranch. And right now, things with me are complicated. I can't take you back to Colorado."

My breath caught in my throat. *What?* "What do you mean? I thought you were here to take me back with you."

He reached for my hand, and I let him take it. "I'm living with my brother and his family right now. It's temporary. But we don't have enough space. And more importantly," he paused, momentarily looked away, then continued, "I don't have the financial means. Things are tight. Really tight."

My head spun. What did he mean by no space and no financial means? What had happened to the man who bought me all of the fake Strawberry Shortcake dolls and shared sales pitches with me? Where was the man who made me feel like I mattered?

I just stood there, numb, not knowing what to say or do. I loved Stan, and I knew he loved me, but I was angry. Angry at him. Angry at Susan. Angry at Robert. I was angry at the world in that moment.

He hugged me and continued with a voice full of emotion, "Even if we're not together in person, Julie, you are always in my heart. You're my daughter, and I'm not going anywhere. I'll still call and check in on you every other week, and you're always welcome to call me anytime. I love you, no matter what."

My heart broke. Yet, I clung to those words. And somehow, I understood that even though my heart was aching, Stan would always be there for me. His love for me was deeper than biology.

Stan had chosen me, then and always. His love for me remained a constant, quiet current running beneath whatever chaos was happening in my life. It was a father's love that was imperfect yet didn't need permission or any explanation. It just was and still is.

Laura stayed quiet for a moment as we continued walking. She took in the surroundings and absorbed the emotion behind my perspective on my relationship with Stan. An exhausted Lily now trailed slightly behind us as we exited the trail and headed the short distance back to the house.

"Julie," Laura said, breaking the short silence. "You were so lucky to have Stan in your life growing up. Do you ever wonder what your life would've been like without his influence?"

"Yes, I do often think about that, and I never miss a chance to tell Stan how appreciative I am that he stayed true to his commitment to me. His consistency in my life—even though we didn't always live together—gave me some semblance of safety in this world. Stan was the only parent that showed me stability and security. When everything else in my world would crack or disappear, he stayed. He was the quiet proof that some mirrors don't shatter. And had Stan not been in my life, I know I wouldn't be the version of me you are talking to today."

"That's incredibly powerful, Julie. I can see how much he means to you," Laura said with a soft smile.

When we arrived at the house, I opened the side door that brought us into the mud room again. I removed my jacket and handed the mini microphone back to Laura. Lily plopped herself down onto the cool, earthy slate floor and gave me a quick thank-you woof.

Laura echoed with her own, "Thank you. I really needed that walk." She then added, "The scenery here is incredible. This world is often filled with so much noise—both around us and inside us—that sometimes, finding peace feels like it's completely out of reach. But not here. If I lived in this part of the country, I could see how I might be more present and centered in my life."

"I agree, Laura. Slowing down in my life and learning to be more aware and present with myself has filtered out a lot of my internal noise. As far as the external goes, I much prefer hearing the soundscape of nature over human-made noise."

SIX

By now, it was late afternoon. The sun was still shining, and the breeze was nonexistent. The temperature hovered around sixty-six degrees, so I suggested we reconvene outside on the deck. We could always wrap up in the deck blankets again if we ended up getting cool.

Laura happily agreed to more time outside, and she grabbed her ginormous tote bag she'd left on the bench earlier. As they walked back across the spacious family room, Laura started to take in the craftsmanship she'd overlooked earlier. As she walked, fixated on the ornate details, she nearly tripped over the largest and most luxurious rug she had ever seen, a blue and ivory antique hand-knotted Oushak rug. She was familiar with the exquisite rugs because her foster father owned a rug business back in New York.

"Laura, are you okay?" I asked with concern.

"All good, Julie. I was too busy looking around and not paying attention to what was right in front of me. Clearly, I need to practice some self-awareness," Laura replied jokingly while catching her breath.

Lily heard the slight rumble of a misstep and darted into the family room. She looked up at Laura with concern and gently licked her hand.

Both women laughed softly as Laura regained her footing.

Laura, Lily, and I stepped out onto the deck, settling into the same seats we occupied earlier that morning. Chef Vincent, anticipating we'd end up there, had already placed a tray of drinks and snacks on the outdoor end table, along with a fresh bowl of water for Lily. Laura once again started her recording app and, with a voice full of curiosity, said, "Okay, Julie. Who's up next?"

David. He was my first husband.

I was seventeen years old. In the summer, my friends and I routinely drove into Kalispell to go dancing at a place called Grizzly's. On the first Saturday of each month, the club hosted a teen night, and in our world, it was the place to be seen. Back then, if you wanted to be visible and connect with other kids, you could cruise around town or go dancing. We liked to do both.

That night at Grizzly's, I spotted a guy dancing on stage with a group of his friends. He moved with such ease. I had never seen a guy dance with such rhythm. It looked like it lived in his body. He exuded confidence rarely found in teenage boys. Once my eyes landed on him, I couldn't look away. He seemed so relaxed and self-assured. He laughed easily, smiled widely, and radiated the kind of joy that made people want to be in his presence. I was hooked.

I leaned over to one of my friends and assertively said, "Who is that guy? I'm going to marry him."

She raised an eyebrow, gave me the classic "sure you are" look, and replied, "Well, you'll never marry him if you don't go meet him. Come on." Before I could protest, she grabbed my hand and dragged me toward the stage. We slipped into the circle of kids he was dancing with, and by the end of the night,

David and I were laughing and moving together in our own little corner of the dance floor.

At the end of the night, when the lights came up, he asked for my number. I could barely believe someone like him would want to hang out with someone like me. As we drove home, I asked my friend, "Do you think he'll call?"

"Oh yeah. He'll call."

And she was right. He called just a few days later, and before long, David and I were inseparable. Five years later, he became husband number one.

David lived on the outskirts of Kalispell, about thirty minutes from where I lived. He was a little taller than me, with sandy blond hair, an athletic build, and a gentleness in his eyes that disarmed everyone. He was kind, sensitive, and wildly creative. He was an incredible painter and had a beautiful singing voice. He loved musical theater and often took center stage in his high school productions.

He had that rare ability to put people at ease. His sense of humor wasn't obnoxious or performative—it was more subtle, a little endearing, and funny as hell. And he had a golden retriever named Daisy, who followed him everywhere. David would speak for her in a sort of silly, falsetto voice, assigning her bits of wisdom that went far beyond her cute little dog years. I loved how he loved her.

His life felt like the opposite of mine. His parents were still married, and they were happy together. They were steady people who welcomed me with open arms. When people describe ideal parents, it's their faces I still picture. He had grown up in the same town his entire life, surrounded by familiarity and continuity. That stability gave him a kind of inner freedom and confidence I didn't understand at the time. He knew who he was—and didn't feel the need to hide it.

I, on the other hand, was a chameleon. If I let myself be seen at all, it was through the lens of who I thought I was supposed to be. I had become an expert at reading the room, shifting myself to fit what I imagined others wanted. At seventeen, I didn't have a clue who I was. I wasn't trying to figure it out either—I was just trying to survive.

Being with David was easy. He didn't make me work for his attention. I was simply included and accepted. He introduced me to a version of life I had never experienced before, one that was consistently safe and happy.

Before David, I only dated boys I didn't really care about. That conscious choice was a form of protection. Keeping people at arm's length was a coping mechanism. I didn't want to get hurt. In our small town, and with my upbringing, detachment was way safer than chasing desire, and to be honest, decent guys were hard to come by.

But David was different.

We dated all summer and into the fall. I fell hard for him. It was terrifying. Saying you're going to marry someone after a crushy dance floor moment is one thing. Feeling it is another. When I started to believe I truly loved him, something inside me panicked.

Slygore whispered, *David doesn't care about you. He was just looking for a piece of ass. You better end this now before he does. You know he's going to leave you. Everyone always does.*

So, in true subconscious sabotage fashion, I blew up our relationship.

We dated for five months before I pulled the ripcord. Honestly, I don't even remember exactly how I made the breakup happen. For whatever reason, my brain filed that memory away in its most distant and forgotten recesses. My guess is that I did something hurtful and unkind.

And, even though I caused the breakup, I was utterly heartbroken.

Our relationship had been different from anything I'd experienced before. David didn't know my family's baggage. He didn't live in my town or hear the whispers about my parents. With David, I was just me—whatever version I showed up in at any moment.

When we split up, I buried that pain. I convinced myself that our relationship and the breakup were both a fluke. Slygore's annoying voice kept taunting me, *Ah ha. See, I was right. You know he never really liked you. You made it all up. You're not worth that kind of love. Everybody hates you. You suck. Go eat worms.* I tried not to hear him and waited for Athena to comfort me, but she stayed silent.

For weeks, I shoved my feelings aside and worked hard to appear fine on the surface. But something in me had shifted. David had shown me a life I hadn't even thought possible. Losing it, even by my own hand, left a quiet ache that followed me.

Months later, I was utterly convinced that David never truly loved me. Slygore, my internal protector, whispered to me repeatedly, and he didn't just suggest it; he made it sound like fact.

But now, with all I've learned over the past years, I see a more complex truth. Slygore wasn't a villain. Instead, he was a firefighter—rushing in to shield me from abandonment, rejection, and vulnerability. Though his actions came across to me as cruel, they were fear's armor—clumsy, yes, but fiercely loyal to my survival.

And David? Well, he wasn't the problem. The idea of being truly loved and then abandoned again terrified me, and that was the problem. My own internal noise drowned out any chance of my being able to trust anyone and the ability to just receive. When I preemptively pushed David away, I created the very outcome I feared. I guess heartbreak on my terms felt safer than being blindsided.

My internal protectors built walls of control around my heart, desperate to keep my tender, wounded parts hidden. If anyone saw those parts of me, I knew I would most likely be rejected, unloved, and left behind.

So clearly, when David got too close, and our connection felt too deep, too safe, too real, Slygore ignited a quick but controlled burn of self-sabotage. He made it really clear that he was the one to listen to, the one I should trust.

Today, I recognize that Athena—my compassionate and wise true self—was deeply buried beneath Slygore's fear at the time. She likely tried to reach me, to whisper guidance, but I just wasn't ready to hear her or believe her.

In September of the following year, I woke with a racing heart and mind from a dream so vivid it nearly jolted me upright in bed. In my dream, something terrible had happened to David. It felt incredibly real. Though David and I hadn't spoken in nearly a year, I couldn't shake the feelings of the dream. So I gathered my courage and awkwardly called his mom.

She was understandably surprised to hear from me, and after a brief pause, she assured me that, as far as she knew, David was fine. She had just spoken with him the day before.

With kindness in her voice, she promised to pass along my message. We chatted briefly, and she asked if I still lived with my grandparents. I replied that Robert had given me a car for graduation and that I recently moved to Missoula. I was now an office assistant at a timber company. I was proud to say that out loud, especially to David's mom. I felt as if I had taken a big step into adulthood.

To my surprise, David called a few days later. He, too, had moved to Missoula and was attending the University of Montana. I thought maybe the Universe was trying to tell me something. We met for coffee a couple of days later, and our conversation flowed as if no time had passed at all. It was easy and without awkwardness or tension. Neither one of us could deny that we still had chemistry. It was like we had taken a pause and picked up where we left off. Whatever cruel thing I did to end our relationship all those months ago was like water under the bridge for him. He had forgiven me—just like that.

Having a dream about David was one thing. But manifesting him back into my life? Well, that was something else entirely. And what exactly was I manifesting? The idea of being truly loved, seen, and then abandoned again still terrified me to my core. But, like many of us, I just stuffed those feelings of fear and anxiety way down inside me, naively assuming they would eventually just go away.

Our friendship had always been easy, light, and genuine. In those early days of reconnecting, we experienced little drama or emotional turbulence. David was as sweet and attentive as ever. He welcomed me back into his life fully and asked for almost nothing in return. It was both beautiful and, at times, disorienting.

Slygore still tried to chime in now and then, *This isn't real. He's going to leave you. You are fooling yourself. You suck, and you should go eat worms.*

But this time, Athena's voice was starting to break through, *You deserve this, Julie. He does love you, and you are worthy of him.*

I didn't always believe her, but I started listening for her voice and her guidance more often. That, in itself, was progress.

Before David, I had unconsciously sought romantic relationships where love had to be earned, proven, or chased. If you've never had to do that, you might not understand how intoxicating it feels to receive love without strings. David opened my eyes to what that kind of love was supposed to feel like—safe, warm, expansive. It was not always comfortable, but it was deeply grounding.

Growing up with so many people drifting in and out of my life, I learned early on how to abandon myself and vanish emotionally in relationships. I had already become so adept at molding myself to fit others' expectations that I often lost sight of who I was. By the time I started dating, I knew how to shape someone else's passions into my passions. Their dislikes became my dislikes. Any boundaries or morals I had faded into the background in exchange for someone's approval.

The thing is, David never required any of that from me. His quiet self-confidence continued to draw me in. Though he didn't know it, his way of being was inspiring me to find my own sense of centeredness. He gave me a radical kind of acceptance, and I wanted to experience that for the rest of my life. It is what led me to marry him.

We got married three years later, just after I turned twenty-two. Like many of us back then, we were young, broke, and optimistic. But we were in love, and for a time, that was more than enough.

David sailed through college in just three years, earning a degree in biology with the kind of quiet determination that came naturally to him. He began searching for a job in his field while I continued climbing the ladder at the timber company. I was promoted to office manager, which brought more responsibility and a modest pay increase. Then, only a few months later, I was offered another promotion. But this one would require me to relocate to Tacoma, Washington.

I loved the thought of moving. I moved so often as a child that I grew accustomed to it, and I liked having a change in scenery. I was excited about experiencing something new, something challenging. My promotion made me feel valued by my boss and the company.

David, on the other hand, had never moved outside of the state of Montana. Montana had been his home for every day of his life. I knew leaving the familiar comforts of his life would stretch his boundaries. But he loved me and agreed without much resistance. He was open to the adventure and looked forward to a new experience.

We packed our modest belongings into our two vehicles and a small U-Haul truck. Our sweet golden retriever, Daisy, jumped into the back seat of David's truck. I got into my car, and off we went, caravanning west. We may not have had much, but we had each other. It felt like a fresh, adult-like kind of start.

In Tacoma, we gradually learned how to create our married life in a tiny two-bedroom cottage with old, creaky wood floors and a fenced-in yard. We did normal everyday things together, like paying bills, cooking dinner, and folding laundry. We explored the city on weekends, discovering cafes, used bookstores, and waterfront hiking trails. We went on grocery runs with Daisy, who got to ride shotgun, and had late-night movie marathons on our brown thrift store couch. Our life was simple, quiet, and steady. It was the first time in my life that I experienced a glimpse of calmness in my body.

Yet, somehow, I simultaneously felt awkward and uneasy. The polarity of those feelings was extremely confusing.

At the time, I didn't have the knowledge or language to articulate what I was feeling or what I was experiencing. I just felt irritated and restless, like there was a low-level hum of anxiety vibrating just beneath the surface of my skin.

It turns out that for a large part of my life, I didn't know I was stuck in something called a functional freeze. On the outside, I looked fine. I was doing all the right things: showing up, getting stuff done, smiling when I needed to. But inside, I was shut down.

Remember me mentioning how I was emotionally numb to a lot of experiences—Susan kicking me out, seeing my biological dad, the death of my grandpa—and how disconnected I was from my body? Well, I eventually learned that was a survival response. It's the nervous system's way of coping when the stress is consistent and never fully stops. You don't necessarily fall apart, but you don't feel fully alive, either. That was me. I got so comfortable in an induced state of detachment that when the stress did finally stop, and no more apparent threats showed up in my life, my body genuinely did not know what to do.

The juxtaposition of finally experiencing stability, safety, and love while not knowing how to receive and relax into it was completely lost on me back then. So, I began to hold my breath, waiting for something to go wrong.

My new role at work came with more responsibility, longer hours, and a pressure I was eager to prove I could handle. Several months after our move, David still had not found a job. He was stuck on figuring out a career that would allow him to utilize his biology degree, and he wasn't willing to settle on something else.

It was scary for me to carry the financial weight of our lives. I was used to the responsibility of taking care of myself, but now the responsibility of taking care of both of us felt like too much. Slygore whispered, *Why are you taking care of David? Shouldn't he be taking care of you? If he really loved you, he'd get off his lazy ass and make some money. He needs to grow up!* I tried unhearing his words, but they stuck with me.

I remember wondering at the time, *Is this how Stan felt? Bearing the weight of our world while Susan and I leaned on him? Did he ever feel afraid under all that responsibility?*

On a clear January afternoon, David, Daisy, and I headed to Point Defiance Park for a walk. We'd fallen in love with this park and its forest trails and water views. We planned to grab lunch afterward at our favorite nearby spot, The Antique Sandwich Company.

As we started our walk and embraced the cold but sunny day, it took me all of five minutes to disrupt the easy silence by blurting, "How's the job search going?"

"I still have some applications out. Haven't heard anything back yet."

"But what do you really want to do? What makes you happy? What kind of work in biology would you be excited to dive into?"

"Honestly, I don't know. I've thought about working with the Forest Service or maybe working with Fish and Wildlife. But I haven't seen anything that jumps out at me."

"What about applying at the zoo? We're right here. We could stop in before heading to lunch just to see what's open."

I knew I had pushed a bit too hard because David slowly turned and gave me a stern look. He said, "Julie, where is this coming from? You've got a great job; it's the whole reason we moved here. The bills are getting paid, and we're happy, right? Why are you pressuring me to do more? We've only been here a few months. I'm actively looking for work. You know that. I've started painting again, and I might also audition for the local theater. I know those aren't jobs, but I'll find something eventually."

What he said made logical sense but didn't soothe my frustration. At that moment, I was also frustrated with myself because my dialogue with David resembled the "find a new job" conversations Susan used to have with Stan. And that made me feel terrible.

David had grown up in a family that always had enough— enough money, enough emotional support, and enough stability. He was shielded from the harsh realities of living without. He wasn't spoiled by any means, but he also didn't know what it was like to be a kid with no heat, an empty fridge, and an absent mom.

Being the only one in our marriage with a steady income was freaking me the hell out. I said in a clipped voice, "David, at some point, you have to grow up and get a job."

The words came out before I could stop them. A momentary silence followed, and I knew instantly Slygore's words had just exited my mouth.

David stopped walking, and his face looked stunned. "Grow up? Did you seriously just say that to me? Julie, who are you right now? This is you and me, not you and your childhood. We're okay. We love each other. We're figuring it out. Why are you so freaked out? We'll ask my parents for help if things don't work out. It's not the end of the world."

But to me, it felt like the end of the world, or at least the end of everything that seemed stable in our lives. "Fine," I snapped back. "Let's just drop it."

I turned away, walking faster, grabbing Daisy's leash from David as if that would release the pressure inside my chest. Slygore was in full swing, jeering and mocking, *Nyah nyah na nyah nyah. You're doing everything, Julie. He's coasting. You're alone in this. You always have been and always will be.*

But then Athena chimed in with her soft, calm voice, *Breathe. This isn't your past. You're safe. You're loved. Everything will be okay.*

After a few more yards, I slowed my pace and my breathing. I turned and waited for David, who walked patiently behind me. I needed peace again, so I reached for David's hand. He took it without hesitation as I said, "I'm sorry. You're right. Let's go have lunch."

At the cafe, we split a bowl of hot soup and a grilled cheese sandwich, then shared a giant slice of carrot cake. It should have been a comforting meal, and it was, in some ways. But as I bit into the last bite of cake, Slygore whispered to me again, *This is your money buying lunch. David's a dreamer, a slacker. You're alone in this.* He was relentless.

One afternoon, Daisy and I went for a walk with our neighbor Kira and her golden retriever, Pippa. Kira was a few years older than me and an ER Psychologist completing an internship at the local hospital. She was grounded, practical, and sharp. I didn't typically open up to people about my childhood or what was really going on inside me, but something about Kira always made me feel safe. And since she was medically trained, I figured she might have some insight into what I often felt but just couldn't quite explain. Kira introduced me to my nervous system.

I started with a softball. "Kira, can I ask you something health-related?" *Duh,* I thought. *Of course, you can. She's your friend, not your doctor. What's she gonna say, No?*

She smiled and said, "Sure, what's up?"

I hesitated, then said, "Okay, I know I've shared a little about my chaotic childhood. And what I'm going to say might sound a little weird, but I think I'm having a nervous breakdown. Lately, I've been feeling on edge. It's as if things with David are too easy, and for some reason, that is making me nervous. And I should be happy, but I'm not and—"

"Okay, I hear you," Kira interjected in an effort to keep me from spiraling. "You said you feel unsettled. Did something happen?"

"No, not particularly. I just feel like I'm not myself. I'm always irritated, even though my life and my marriage are really good right now. What is happening to me?"

"Ah, I understand. It's possible your nervous system, because of the trauma you experienced growing up, isn't regulated or balanced. Do you know anything about the nervous system?

"No. Not a thing," I muttered, embarrassed.

"It's okay. Most people don't know. It's a shame our schools don't teach this stuff, Julie. It's life-changing when you truly understand how your nervous system works and how to keep it balanced and stable. I'll keep it light, but stop me if I get too far into the science."

I nodded for her to continue.

"The nervous system is divided into two main branches, the central nervous system, or CNS, and the peripheral nervous system, or PNS. Each has its subdivisions, but the one I think matters most for your description is the autonomic nervous system, also known as your ANS. And yes, I already know you're dying to make a joke about ANS sounding like anus, aren't you?"

Like a little kid, I tried not to smile, but I couldn't hold it in. "Yup. Sorry, Kira. It does sound like you said anus." I giggled. "Please, continue."

Kira rolled her eyes and continued, "The A . . . N . . . S controls your involuntary functions—like your heartbeat, digestion, and breathing. It has three main parts: the enteric, sympathetic, and parasympathetic nervous systems. The enteric nervous system is essentially your gut brain. It's made up of neurons in your digestive tract. While that may not sound exciting, it actually produces a huge percentage of your feel-good chemicals—somewhere between 85 and 97 percent of your serotonin and around 50 percent of your dopamine."

"Wait, so my gut literally makes me feel happy or anxious?"

"Pretty much, yeah. Then there's the sympathetic nervous system—your fight, flight, freeze, or fawn response. It's built to protect you. And the parasympathetic system is the opposite.

It kicks in when you feel safe. That's your rest-and-digest mode."

I nodded slowly, starting to see where she was going.

"When you're in a healthy, balanced state, your nervous system naturally moves back and forth between those two—sympathetic and parasympathetic—every few hours. But for you, being raised with chaos and experiencing so much chronic stress, your body likely became more accustomed to being in its sympathetic mode. When you're constantly on guard and looking out for danger, your nervous system gets flooded with cortisol and adrenaline. And over time, that becomes your baseline."

I raised my eyebrows. "So basically, I've been marinating in stress hormones since the age of two?"

She gave a soft smile. "It's quite possible and might explain what you're feeling. And because of that, when your environment finally is calm—when there's no drama, no threat—your body doesn't recognize it as safe. It feels foreign. Unsafe, even. Your body craves the hormones it's been used to. And none of this is conscious. It's all biological."

I thought about that a moment, then said, "So what you're saying is that when my life resembles safety and security and contains far less stress, I would still need a constant IV drip of adrenaline and cortisol to keep my nervous system feeling safe because that's what it is used to? Is that right? Is there any chance you can hook me up?"

She laughed. "Um, no. And trust me, you don't want that IV drip. Too much cortisol disrupts mood, sleep, digestion, and heart rate. It actually causes exhaustion. It's why so many people feel overwhelmed, anxious, and irritable."

"Ah, that makes sense. So what do I do instead?" I asked, half-joking, half-desperate.

"Well," she said gently, "you start by noticing, being more aware. Then, you can start practicing ways to intentionally calm your nervous system. Try practicing deep breathing, mindfulness, gratitude, or whatever helps you return to your center. And consistently remind yourself that peace doesn't mean danger. You're safe now."

Spoken like Athena, I thought. "That's fascinating, Kira. I feel a little better knowing that something isn't physically wrong with me. Thank you."

"Nope, you're not broken. And you're welcome," she said. "Now, every time I describe the nervous system to a patient, I'm probably going to chuckle, internally, of course, when I talk about the ANS. Only you could make that kind of connection, Julie. Good gracious." Kira winked and smiled.

"Yep, I am a pillar of emotional maturity—until someone casually drops the word anus, and then it's all over. Honestly, it's a miracle I'm allowed to sign legal documents." I replied with a short, sharp laugh.

We finished the walk in a happy, companionable silence, Daisy and Pippa trotting side by side, tails wagging. Kira waved as we parted ways, and I found myself breathing a little more easily. I didn't have it all figured out yet—heck, I wasn't even sure I fully grasped all of Kira's sciencey stuff—but I was beginning to understand what might be happening inside me.

My body wasn't betraying me. It was simply doing what it had learned to do. Just like Slygore, my nervous system was protecting me, even when I no longer needed protection.

Even with this rational understanding of my nervous system, my mind and body had other plans. It knew exactly what to do to keep me in familiar territory. It knew how to mix the right cocktail of adrenaline and cortisol to make me feel alert, prepared, and alive.

And Slygore didn't want the deep breathing and gratitude. Please. That was for lightweights. He wanted the buzz of vigilance, the edge of control. Movement and busyness are what he prescribed. And Slygore, ever devoted, knew he needed to stay center stage.

A few days later, while David was out playing lacrosse with some of his friends, Slygore chimed in out of nowhere, *This marriage is too easy. Julie. David can't be the right person if it's this easy. Marriage is supposed to be hard. Where's the work? Where's the struggle? Real couples fight, and he rarely fights with you. That's not normal. Something's off. You're too happy. And happy means comfortable. Comfortable means unprepared. You're going to be blindsided, just like always.*

I desperately tried tuning him out, but it was impossible. He just kept going, and it was wearing me down.

You'll be devastated when he leaves, and he'll leave. So get ahead of it. What were you thinking, letting someone in? You don't deserve this kind of happiness. David feels more like a friend than he does a husband, doesn't he? This isn't a real marriage, and you know it. Come on, Julie. You've always known this wouldn't last. And don't forget about the fact that you can't have kids. I've been telling you this for years. David wants them. Do him a favor and end this before you really get hurt again.

Slygore's internal barrage of fear, disguised as logic, was unsettling. His voice, though exhausting, was also extremely persuasive. Was he right? I thought, *No, this is just my brain trying to protect me.* But maybe what he said was true. What if

I'm just not seeing it? Like with Susan. I didn't see that coming. *Okay, stop. Just stop all of the thinking, Julie.*

I took a deep breath and muttered aloud, "Slygore, shut the hell up." Simultaneously, I could almost feel that IV drip starting again.

That following week, on another walk with Kira, I brought up my endless spinning thoughts. My monkey mind, as Kira called it.

She listened quietly as I talked. Her expression was soft and patient. Then she said something that stuck. "What you're describing is known as cognitive distortion. In other words, your brain sends you seemingly endless negative thoughts that are not grounded in reality. Imagine it like your mind making up stories that sound like truth but aren't true. These thought patterns come from fear and trauma, and they're intended for self-protection. Worst of all, these distortions trick you into believing the world is more threatening than it actually is."

I walked quietly for a few steps, trying to grasp what she said. Then I asked, "Okay, but how can I tell if I'm responding to a distortion or reality?"

"That's the hard part. Learning to question your thoughts is essential, especially the ones that make you feel small, unworthy, or afraid."

Wow, I thought to myself, *how am I supposed to keep all this stuff straight?* And even though I nodded as if I understood, the truth was I didn't understand any of what Kira was telling me. I felt stupid. I lacked the skills and emotional bandwidth to integrate any of what I had just learned. And honestly, I struggled to see how it all applied to me. I then wondered, *Maybe Slygore was a distortion?*

She tried to reassure me. "Everyone experiences these distortions. It's part of being human. They come along most often when you're feeling low or vulnerable. The trick is to notice them and avoid giving them any power."

I nodded again. And I wanted to notice them. I wanted to feel better in my body. However, the truth was that I believed I had already given away my power a long time ago.

From the outside, I appeared to have every reason to be happy. I had a kind husband, a safe home, and a quiet life. But as the days and months continued, I felt more and more trapped—not by David, but by the noise in my own head. This easy, peaceful life triggered anxiety in me. My nervous system didn't yet recognize calm as safe—it just knew it was unfamiliar. This was such a big part of why the calmness of my life felt unsettling; I had been living in survival mode for so long. I genuinely felt like I was going crazy.

The distorted thoughts kept rolling in, unchecked and unchallenged. My thoughts were conditioned fears making noise, but they appeared to me like truth. Eventually, I gave up trying to fight and simply began to believe them. And once I believed the thoughts, everything changed.

My perception of our relationship began to twist, conforming to match my constructed narrative. The lens through which I now saw David, our marriage, and myself had become warped. And I didn't even realize it.

Nothing had changed between us, but everything had changed within me.

One gorgeous sunny Sunday afternoon, David, Daisy, and I were stuck in traffic, inching our way back home after a delightful hike near Mount Rainier. David's relaxed arm draped casually over the steering wheel. Daisy was curled up in the back seat, napping. And I was staring out the window, watching the trees blur into one another, again wondering why I felt so numb.

"Hey, Julie," David said, breaking the quiet. "I want to talk to you about something."

Uh oh. I know that tone. I turned toward him with a practiced smile on my face and asked, "What's up?"

He glanced at me, hesitant but sincere. "We've never really talked about having kids. What would you think about getting serious about trying to have a baby?"

"Oh." I was caught entirely off guard. I could feel the warmth of the day draining from my body. "Well, um, I guess so. But work is pretty demanding right now. Maybe we could wait a little while?"

By then, David had picked up a full-time job as a stock manager at a local grocery store. It wasn't glamorous, but it covered part of the bills. It also left him with plenty of time for pick-up lacrosse games, painting in the afternoons, and rehearsing for local theater productions. He had free time and was quite content. I, on the other hand, felt trapped in a career with pressure, expectations, a larger paycheck, and the looming intuition that I was barren.

David nodded thoughtfully, unfazed. "Well, we're in our mid-twenties. Your mom had you when she was nineteen. My mom was twenty-three. Daisy is basically our starter kid. It just seems like the next step for us."

His voice was tender, hopeful. But I wasn't hearing David anymore. I was hearing Slygore's immediate rant, *You know you can't have kids. Your body is broken, just like you. It's a miracle you were even born. When he finds out, he's gonna leave. He's just waiting for a reason. Go on, tell him. I dare you.*

I wanted to shove my fingers in my ears and scream just to silence the noise. But I couldn't. So, instead, I forced brightness into my voice and said, "You're right. We can start trying. If that's what you really want, we'll do it."

You suck. You can't even tell him the truth, Slygore sneered. *He'll leave you soon. Just you wait and see.* I felt sick to my stomach.

Later that night, I thought back to something Kira had told me during one of our walks—about the brain's wiring and neuroplasticity. "When neurons fire together, they wire together," she'd said. The brain learns from repeated experience, and it changes accordingly. Sometimes, those changes help you heal. And sometimes, they reinforce your unwanted patterns and behaviors.

The question I asked myself was, how in the world did I manage to create this intricate, tangled web of beliefs, and how can I undo all of it? My uphill battle wasn't just with myself; it was with Slygore. It was with my brain, my nervous system, Susan, Robert, and all of the chaos from my childhood. My perceived battles were becoming overwhelming, and I was desperate to escape the mounting pressure.

By our third year of marriage, Slygore was a constant companion. He spoke, and I obeyed. His logic, though flawed, became the soundtrack of my inner life. He promised protection. He swore that emotional distance would prevent abandonment. He told me it was safer to be lonely than vulnerable. I believed him.

His whispers gradually rewired my thinking until my nervous system scanned for danger, even within David's kindness. I began to mistake his gentleness for weakness and his steadiness for stagnation.

I heard faint whispers from Athena on occasion, *You are safe. You are loved.* But most of the time, her gentle truths fell on deaf ears. She was no match for Slygore's misguided wisdom.

I wanted to love David fully. I wanted connection, intimacy, and partnership. But I didn't know how to experience those things without fear that they'd be ripped away from me. Love wasn't modeled for me in a healthy way. I didn't know how to trust it once I had it. So, instead of leaning in, I pulled away.

I didn't know that past experiences didn't have to dictate future outcomes. All I knew was that if Susan could discard me, anyone could—even David. And I wasn't going to let that happen again.

So, over the next twelve months, I armored up. I smiled when I didn't feel like smiling. I withheld pieces of myself that initially came so freely. And created just enough space so that if things fell apart, maybe, just maybe, I wouldn't fall apart, too. I thought I was protecting myself from heartbreak, but in truth, I was building the very path that would lead me there.

The affection and playfulness that were once part of our intimacy disappeared. We went through the routine of trying to conceive, and I kept up the appearance of disappointment and surprise each month when the at-home tests came back negative. I knew I didn't deserve to have kids, but David shouldn't have had to deal with my infertility. Sounding like a mirror image of Slygore, I could almost hear myself saying, *I suck; I'd better go eat worms.*

David, Daisy, and I were in the living room one Sunday afternoon. David relaxed into the comfortable cushions of the worn leather armchair. Daisy was curled up in her fluffy bed, which rested on the rug nearby.

I stood by the window with my arms crossed. My eyes weren't really seeing anything on the other side of the glass. I said in a voice devoid of emotion, "I can't do this anymore, David. This charade is exhausting."

I couldn't see his face but could hear his posture shift in the chair. Softly, he asked, "What charade, Julie? What are you talking about?"

I turned to face him and said, "Pretending we're a happy couple and waiting for a baby that's never coming. I'm tired of trying. Tired of failing. You act like none of this is a big deal. You never get upset. You never fight with me."

He looked genuinely confused, and who could blame him? I, too, was confused by what I was feeling. He asked, "Is that what you want? For us to fight?"

"I want something real, David." I began to pace and said, "I need someone who takes life seriously. Someone who's not painting, playing lacrosse, or rehearsing for some community play every night." My words oozed resentment. But beneath all of that was my sincere belief that I wasn't worthy of him or our life together.

David sat still for a moment, then stood slowly, his eyes never leaving mine. "Julie, I've tried so hard to give you space. I've done everything I know how to do to be here for you, but I can't keep guessing. I feel like you're pushing me away, and I don't know why." He paused. "If this is about the job, I'll find something else. If it's about the baby, we can stop trying. We can adopt if that's what it takes."

"It's not about the job. Or a baby." I wrapped my arms around myself, barely holding it together. "It's everything. I can't be who you need me to be. I don't know how to be kind. I'm angry all the time. And the worst part is that I can't stand how kind you are to me. I don't deserve any of it." I was rambling, and it probably sounded like I was on hallucinogenic drugs. To be honest, I wish I had been; that might have offered a valid excuse for my behavior.

I turned away before seeing his reaction and walked into the kitchen. As soon as he was out of sight, the tears came.

Back in the living room, David crouched beside Daisy, stroking her soft fur. His shoulders slumped as the weight of realization hit him—he could finally see just how high the wall between us had grown. "Come on, girl," he whispered to Daisy as he motioned for her to get up. "Let's go for a walk. I think your mom needs some time to herself."

I watched the two of them walk out the door and quickly disappear down the street from the kitchen window. I knew, and I think he knew; it was the beginning of our end.

Four more months passed, and I buried myself in work, using it as both a shield and a sword. Amidst pleasantries and the routine of daily life, I continued randomly sabotaging our connection, one sarcastic comment, one cold shoulder at a time, until I finally asked David for a divorce.

I felt awful inside my body, and I felt like a terrible human being. Yet I had succeeded in controlling the disappointment, the loss, and how it would all end this time. I was so detached by then that I told myself I was just protecting us both from the greater pain of him eventually walking away. This was how I justified ending our marriage.

By the time I sat across from him and said, "I want out," David didn't fight. He looked tired. Worn out. I knew this wasn't what he wanted, and he would've stopped it if he could have, but I think he had already mourned the loss of us by then. I had become someone unrecognizable to him, but the barrier around my heart, the fear of being left, and the idea of not being enough were all too familiar to me.

Our divorce was finalized just after my twenty-sixth birthday. I didn't take many of our possessions and didn't put up a fight when David asked to keep Daisy. I felt like that was the least I could do for him, especially since she was his dog first.

It wasn't until decades later that I realized David had been a mirror for me—the first mirror—showing me the parts of myself I couldn't find the courage to see. His love was steady, honest, and open. It was never guarded, shaped by fear, or constantly waiting for the inevitable abandonment. In his presence, I was invited to see what love could be, and I declined the invitation.

I missed another thing back then, too. A pattern was forming within me, the same pattern I had despised in Susan. It was the survival strategy of creating emotional distance and finding a reason to leave people when they got too close. I think it was her way of staying safe and in control, and it was progressively becoming my pattern, too.

David showed me love without distortion. I just didn't believe the image was mine. His greatest gift to me wasn't our marriage—but the clarity it eventually gave me.

Over the years, we have crossed paths a handful of times. He remarried over twenty years ago and has two now adult children. He seems truly happy. We've exchanged occasional emails and a kind word here and there. We're not friends, exactly, but we're not strangers either.

Looking back at the young woman I was, I don't feel judgment for her. I feel compassion. I want to wrap her in my arms and whisper, *You are safe now. You are worthy of love.*

Bringing myself back into the present moment, I looked down at my watch and was surprised to see that it was nearly 5:30 p.m. "Wow, I can't believe the time. I hope I didn't keep you from any other obligations," I said to Laura.

Laura stopped the recording device and put her notebook down on the adjacent table. "No, not at all," she answered. "I flew in last night just for this interview and don't know anyone else in town other than you. I was planning to go back to my hotel, grab dinner at the hotel restaurant, and get to bed early. The three-hour time difference is catching up with me today. But again, you weren't keeping me from anything."

"Okay. That's good. I'm glad," I said with a long sigh.

Laura continued, "So, tomorrow. Let's have a game plan. I'm headed to Los Angeles late tomorrow night to interview Debbie Gardner. She is the founder of Bridges Beyond Bars, the nonprofit that empowers formerly incarcerated women through culinary training and employment opportunities. I believe you two have met? I think my flight is at 8:15 p.m., so we should have plenty of time for the rest of your story." Laura took a brief pause to look at her phone's calendar, then asked, "What time would you like to get started in the morning?"

"Yes, I do know Debbie. She is a wonderfully kind person, and her organization has made a massive impact on so many women. I feel honored to be in such great company." I smiled and couldn't help but feel gratitude for the moment. "Would a 9 a.m. start work for you?"

"Perfect," Laura replied enthusiastically. "I look forward to hearing the rest of your story tomorrow, Julie. And again, thank you for being so vulnerable and open with me. I've had a great time today and have enjoyed hearing about your life. I appreciate you opening up your home to me and sharing the magic of this place, too."

"You are more than welcome, Laura. I've enjoyed your company as well, and from the looks of it, so has Lily." I pointed to where Lily was sprawled out across Laura's overflowing tote bag.

Laura's entire face formed a smile as she looked down. She hesitated, unwilling to disturb Lily. "Looks like I'll be sleeping right here tonight. She's too cute to wake. I can't do it." She teased.

As Laura briefly pondered how to regain possession of her bag, a squirrel ran up one of the side beams of the house, leaped onto the deck, and ran over Lily's back leg. Lily, who was quite startled, sprang to her feet like a bolt of lightning, knocking over her water bowl in the process. The squirrel jumped onto another cross beam and fled the scene.

"What in the world just happened?" Laura shrieked.

With great reverence and the largest smile of the day, I answered, "The Universe. That's what just happened. It let you off the hook, so you didn't have to be the one to disturb sweet Lily."

"Ah, I like it. Thank you, Universe. That was very helpful. And creative, I might add," Laura said as she collected her notebook and huge tote bag.

I walked Laura to the front door, returning to the same spot where we first met that morning. It had been a full day, and the emotion of everything I shared lingered in the air.

With Lily by my side, I said in a soft voice, "Goodnight, Laura. Drive safely, and we will see you in the morning."

"Goodnight, Julie. Thank you," Laura responded, already halfway out the door.

SEVEN

The next morning, I woke to Lily's cold, wet nose hovering near my face; it was 5 a.m. and time for breakfast. Most often, we'd start our day well before the sun came up. This always gave me ample time to complete my daily routine—including yoga, mantra, and meditation—and still have time left over to enjoy a walk with Lily. Today, our trail walk along the bay began with a beautiful sunrise, but rain clouds started rolling in not long after the sun came up. The light of the morning dimmed as the sky turned gray; the weather was shifting gears again.

My husband, Todd, who occasionally joined us on our morning walks, was still out of town visiting his sister, Amy. Amy, whom I affectionately refer to as my "gift-sister," lives in Montana. The two of us have become close over the years. I hated missing out on an opportunity to see her, but the interview with Laura had been planned well in advance.

After our walk, Lily followed me into my office. I looked over my calendar, set my intention for the day, and took a quick phone call. As I was wrapping up my conversation with the executive director at Girls Rise and Shine, Chef Vincent quietly entered the office carrying a tray with assorted teas, a carafe of coffee, and some freshly baked pastries. The mingling aromas infused the room.

"I thought you and Laura might want to meet here in your office this morning. It started drizzling outside a few minutes ago," he said.

"Yes. Good call, Vincent. Thank you. Here in my office will be just fine. Lily and I saw a beautiful sunrise on our walk this morning before the clouds rolled in, didn't we, Miss Silly Lily? You are a good girl, aren't you?" I said in a high cartoon voice as I looked in Lily's direction. Lily wagged her tail proudly.

Chef Vincent set the tray on a tall, wooden credenza made of Macassar ebony that stretched nearly the length of the wall. On top were neatly arranged objects that signaled success: a sculptural lamp, an exotic plant, and two ornately carved imperial jade statues. The credenza and its collection weren't just knickknacks; they made a statement.

As he turned to leave, Chef Vincent asked, "Julie, do you have any preferences for lunch?"

"Everything you make is incredible. Whatever menu you create will be just fine. I appreciate all you do here."

"Thank you, Julie," Chef Vincent said as he exited the room and headed toward the kitchen.

It was nearly 9 a.m. when I heard the doorbell. I made my way to the grand foyer and swung open the large wood doors, which let in a gust of wind and splashing drops of water. The drizzle had turned to gentle rain. Laura greeted me with a smile and her disheveled, overflowing tote bag.

"Good morning, Laura. Come on in. I hope your drive here this morning wasn't too chaotic with the rain."

"Good morning. The drive was fine. I'm glad Mother Earth waited until I was nearly to your front door before she opened up the skies."

"We try to keep the sunny, beautiful days you experienced yesterday down to a minimum. We can't have everyone moving here and spoiling it for the rest of us, now can we?"

Laura removed her damp coat and shoes and set them in the mud room. Hearing Laura's voice, Lily bounced over, ears flopping and tail joyfully wagging. Laura's face lit up when she saw the sweet Labrador. Lily then leaned her entire body against Laura's legs, desiring a few scratches behind her ear.

Laura obliged and said, "Good morning, Miss Lily. It's a pleasure to see you again, too."

I grinned as I watched the interaction between the two of them. "We'll use my office this morning if that's comfortable for you."

"Yes, that's perfect. I'm glad you didn't suggest meeting out on your deck. I didn't bring my wetsuit."

I flashed her a smile and bantered back, "Oh, don't worry. I have one you could've borrowed." We laughed, easy with each other's company, as we walked down the long, open hallway to my office. Laura and her travel command center of a tote bag followed slowly as she admired the photographic art on the walls, being careful not to trip over anything this time.

When we arrived at the office, I offered Laura some coffee, tea, and the delicate pastries Chef Vincent had prepared. Once we had both selected what we wanted to eat and drink, we returned to the same seats we used the day before.

Laura sank into the generously sized leather chair, and Lily snuggled up next to her feet with her favorite stuffie and began to doze off.

From her huge bag, Laura pulled out the items she needed to begin, careful not to disrupt the disorganized chaos within the cavernous space. She made her adjustments, started her recording app, and settled into her chair. "This is Laura Carrington. Day two of my interview with Julie Sloan."

I took a long, deep breath in, slowly let it out, and gazed out the window. Then I began. I left off yesterday with David, my first husband, and my first true invitation for self-awareness in a romantic relationship. The next opportunity I had to confront my internal struggles was with Brian. He was my second husband.

Though I initiated the divorce from David, months later, I still felt overwhelming guilt and sadness. I truly loved him, and now I felt destined to spend the rest of my pathetic life alone. At the time, I often thought, *I suck and I should just become a nun.* I know that sounds dramatic, but I was very dramatic at that age. The single life wasn't what I had envisioned, that's for sure. I grieved for David. In retrospect, pushing him away felt like a very compulsive decision.

I was twenty-six and single. In addition to missing David's presence, I was also feeling the financial pinch of living alone. Though my job paid me well, David and I racked up some credit card debt, and my old car was no longer reliable, so I needed a new one.

The divorce had left a dark space inside me that I desperately wanted to avoid. So, I filled it by enrolling in part-time accounting classes at the local college—it was my first time attending classes beyond high school. I found a shared apartment with a pretty water view in Des Moines, Washington, which split the distance between my office job and the college. When I wasn't working or in class, I spent a lot of my time at the marina-front bar at Anthony's restaurant. I loved watching the running lights of boats blur into the twilight and chatting with the onslaught of tourists.

I was an assistant operations manager at the timber company by day and a lonely student by night. I had excelled at work, but Slygore always offered a constant stream of sabotage to remind me just who I was. *You'll never find love again. You're nothing. No one will ever love you. You suck.* In those moments, I wistfully wondered what I'd tossed away. Admittedly, I had regrets. My heart ached for both David and Daisy.

Brian was a manager at the restaurant, and the bar was his area of responsibility. He seemed to be on shift every time I went to the bar. He did not appear to be my type at all. He had a medium build, was a few years younger, and carried a reserve that bordered on an odd mixture of confidence and aloofness. He always moved through the dining room with a focused energy, offering a brief but friendly word for each table and longer hellos to the bar regulars. He once casually mentioned to me that he worked sixty-hour weeks, which made my own carefully constructed life feel pretty flimsy.

After a few minutes of casual conversation one evening, he said, "I absolutely love my job." His eyes lit up with a strange, almost unsettling enthusiasm. He followed by saying he was put on this earth to work and serve others by helping them have a memorable experience. He sounded like he was quoting some first-day training manual. I thought it was odd to love a job as a restaurant bar manager, but who was I to judge? Although, I did.

I didn't see him as dating material, but he seemed nice enough to get to know me as a friend. I once asked him to join me and a couple of other friends for a drink at a different bar on his day off. He declined, saying he didn't drink. He wasn't a party kind of guy. I even invited him on a hike at Salt Water State Park with a few others and me. He replied, "No, thank you. I don't do hikes." *What in the hell does this guy like to do?* I thought.

Though he seemed kind, he mostly preferred to keep a professional distance from all the other regular restaurant patrons and me. He took his job very seriously, and his lack of interest in socializing with me, in particular, felt like an intriguing challenge. Brian's dedication to his career and his aloofness were slowly becoming more attractive to me.

Interesting, right? Unknowingly, at the time, I saw Brian's lack of interest in me as an attractive quality. You see, I had rejected David, in part, because I felt like he was far too nice to me. I didn't believe I deserved his love and his kindness. The problem was that I wanted to find someone to love again, but just not entirely. That was far too risky. So, my brain made a likely suggestion. I should be with a man who wouldn't make me his priority in life—problem solved!

This indifference strategy, as I called it, was familiar to me and easy to read. I would recognize all the warning signs to look for when things started to decline because it was reminiscent of my relationship with Susan. And because I knew how to navigate things when Susan withheld her attention, I also knew what to do and how to behave to receive her love. My brain was telling me that this was my solution to finding love. I needed something more familiar, and the indifference strategy proved to be the key.

As the weeks passed and my new, unconscious love strategy was in place, I began to appreciate Brian's energetic presence and physical appearance. He, in turn, began to notice my interest in him. I was also drawn to his ambition, a trait that David visibly seemed to lack.

Ultimately, Brian and I began dating. However, because fraternizing with patrons was frowned upon, we kept our relationship hidden from his boss and the rest of the restaurant staff. Brian didn't want to risk getting fired; his job was his priority. Over the following months, we pretended to be platonic in public. Even the couple of women I hung out with at the bar didn't know we were together. It was fun being mysterious and keeping our secret from the world. The secretness of our relationship added an element of heightened excitement and anticipation, fueling our connection.

One evening, when we were cozied up on his couch, Brian said, "Hey, babe, I was offered a promotion to general manager today."

I hugged him and said, "Wow! Congratulations! That's great news!"

"Thanks! But there's a catch. The new GM position is in Bend, Oregon, where I grew up. It's a great opportunity, and I'd love to move back there. What would you say about moving there with me? I think you'd love it. Plus, in Bend, we can start our life as a couple and won't have to sneak around anymore. What do you think?"

Before I could answer him, Brian said, "I'll earn enough money so we can get a small place together, and you can take your time looking for work. If you still want to work at a timber company, I know a few around there. Or you can branch into something else. It's gonna be great! You're going to love my family. What do you think?" This time, he paused so I could reply.

At first, the words, "I'll earn enough money so we can get a small place together, and you can take your time looking for work," sounded eerily familiar. I said almost those exact same words to David when I got a promotion and wanted us to move for my job. *Huh, how odd*, I thought. If the Universe was trying to tell me something, I certainly wasn't listening.

I knew Brian was eager to please at work and wanted to accelerate his early career. I also knew I wasn't the type of person who would just sit around and wait for the perfect job. Plus, moving again sounded fun. It would be a fresh new start with Brian. I gave little thought to what I wanted for my own life—career or otherwise. In hindsight, I see I was far too willing to quit school and leave a stable job where I had routinely received praise for my work.

I loved Brian at the time, don't get me wrong. But I don't know if I loved him enough to give up my life and move for him. I think that at the time, his offer probably felt like it was the culmination of all the challenge, anticipation, and mystery of our relationship. I was caught up in the drama of it all and was likely shocked that Brian, or anyone for that matter, wanted to be with me.

So, with virtually no resistance on my part, I enthusiastically said, "Yes! Let's do it!" Almost immediately, Slygore chimed in, *This is never going to work. He doesn't really love you. He just thinks he does. He loves his job. You'll never come first. You suck anyway. Nobody likes you.*

Bend, Oregon, was beautiful. I loved it there, and Brian's family was amazing. His parents seemed genuinely happy to have him living back in town. Brian and I found a simple split-level, three-bedroom home to rent not too far from downtown, and I found a well-paying sales job with an electronics company. Brian was working his typical restaurant manager, sixty-hour work weeks, which left me with time to explore the city and get to know his family. A few months into our new life together, things were good. I still wasn't feeling major sparks for Brian, but our life was easy, and we were happy. Chaos and drama were nowhere near, and it felt good—for a while.

And now is when you'll see my pattern emerge. Anytime my life became too settled, too easy, and too comfortable, my nervous system told my body that something was off. Remember my conversation with Kira about the constant IV drip? When trauma and chaos, which is essentially anything that is too much, too soon, or too fast, weren't present in my life, my body didn't know how to react. It was disorienting and unfamiliar. This explains why I created drama with David and then divorced him. It explains why I wanted to chase Brian, move, find a new job . . . I could keep going, but I'm sure my point is clear.

Essentially, it is the inverse of the ideal human nervous system function. Although, due to the levels of stress and turmoil in the world, many people function this way today.

Imagine you had a friend who grew up in a rural setting but took a job on a military base, which was a bustling training center for helicopter pilots. It was a loud and noisy place at first, uncomfortable even. After a few months, the constant thumping of rotor blades overhead became more familiar. That noise, which was once very jarring, turned into a kind of background comfort for her nervous system. It was what she knew.

Now, whenever she returns to her rural home for a visit, the sudden absence of that noise leaves her feeling disoriented and dysregulated without it. Working in that environment—with the helicopters and the chaos—trained her nervous system to feel at ease with unpredictability. So when life isn't noisy or chaotic, like when she goes back home, it actually feels unfamiliar and uncomfortable. And all of this happens subconsciously.

Only through self-awareness can this pattern be changed. I didn't have that self-awareness when Brian proposed to me about six months after living in Bend. I genuinely thought Brian was my last and only opportunity to find love. He was handsome and kind. He had a great job, and he loved me. What else did I need? I told myself that after we married, that spark that was missing for me would eventually show up.

The weather on our wedding day was picture-perfect. The scent of sweet pine and vanilla filled the air, gently reminding me of Montana. We had a small ceremony. The church pews primarily held Brian's friends and family. A few of my friends from Montana attended, along with Stan and his new wife. Robert wasn't there because I honestly forgot to invite him.

As I stood in the hallway outside the sanctuary that day, waiting to walk down the aisle, I heard Athena's calm voice clearly saying, *Don't do this, Julie. This is a mistake.* Hang on a minute. I thought Athena was my voice of comfort and support. Why the heck was she telling me to call it off? Slygore, the usual harbinger of doom, was oddly silent. Call off the wedding? I couldn't do that. Yes, I had the jitters and a large pit in my stomach, but I couldn't walk away.

I disregarded Athena's advice and followed my own. As the wedding march swelled and the expectant faces of our family and friends turned toward me, I took a quick, shallow breath and stepped forward, disregarding my heightened unease.

At twenty-eight, part of me was scared to be alone. Another part of me was holding on too tightly to what other people thought of me. I was more comfortable disappointing myself than I was inconveniencing someone else. I thought my intuition was illogical, so I didn't trust it. If I had been fully honest with myself and known who I was back then, I would have honored those feelings and embraced my emotions—especially on my wedding day.

But in my irrational mind, I believed being me caused Susan to kick me off the ranch at fifteen. Being me also led to being a divorcee at twenty-six. My brain told me I needed to be someone other than me, and I didn't know how to do that either. Not only did I believe I was unworthy of love, but I also believed that safety and security came only when I pretended to be someone other than who I was. A lot of anxiety came with that belief. So, for the second time, I entered a marriage feeling like I was not enough.

After starting our married lives in Bend, Brian was scouted for another position in Boise, Idaho. We took the leap of faith, packed everything up again, and moved six hours east. Moving and re-establishing myself in another city was clearly not an issue for me as an adult—a nice bonus from my childhood—but it was a big deal for Brian. I seemed to have a knack for marrying men who had a homegrown, stable, and loving upbringing.

It's a subconscious kind of emotional magnetism. Like getting close to someone who came from that world would help me feel some of what I missed in my childhood. Well, stable home life or not, Brian's parents practically disowned him when he told them we were leaving Bend, to the point where he almost declined the job offer.

I believed in Brian and supported every career move he made, even though it meant I had to start over and find a new job each time we relocated. I knew how much his professional success meant to him, and somewhere along the way, I stopped prioritizing my own career. I wanted a fulfilling professional life, too, but I ended up placing more value on Brian's ambitions than my own. We followed his career path, not mine.

I could always find a decent job in office management or accounting. I was good at it, but starting over every couple of years wasn't really what I wanted from my life. I used to wonder where I would've been in my career with the timber company back in Washington had I stayed there and not followed Brian to Oregon.

I honestly didn't know if that's what being in a healthy marriage looked like. I had so many questions and no satisfying answers. Did most wives support their husbands' careers above their own? Was that a normal sacrifice? Surely, I had goals and ambitions of my own, but what exactly were they? And did my aspirations even matter if we perpetually moved from city to city for Brian's job? At the time, I felt a bit hopeless, as if I was a victim of my decisions.

Aside from the noise in my head and my lingering, unanswered questions, our life together in Boise was relatively uneventful. But I was very lonely. Brian worked six, sometimes seven days a week, usually ten to twelve hours a day. I spent a lot of my evenings and weekends alone or with a very exhausted husband. I had few friends, my job wasn't the most satisfying, and we didn't even have a dog to keep me company.

At the time, I didn't have the capacity to even notice the anxiousness building in my body, but I was acutely aware that I was feeling quite irrelevant in the world. I hated that feeling and desperately wanted to get rid of it. I needed to redirect that energy into something else. The one thing I could do consistently and well was support Brian and his goals. I decided to focus on being the quintessential "good wife." It was an easy way to avoid acknowledging my perceived worthlessness.

It wasn't long before Brian received yet another promotion that moved us back to Des Moines, Washington. We found a brand-new apartment on the southern end of town that had huge floor-to-ceiling windows in the family room. You could see Mt. Rainer and the marina. To me, that was one of the best parts of moving back to the area, being near the ocean. Brian continued to work sixty to seventy hours a week, and I found another random job. The timber company I used to work for was now owned by a larger national company, so it no longer had the same appeal it did years prior.

I had also lost touch with many of the people I knew from Des Moines, which meant I was still spending much of my time alone. I knew it was only a matter of time until Brian got transferred again, and this time, I just didn't have the energy to make new friends. I was becoming tired. My whole life had been spent in motion—reacting, fixing, proving. I wanted to feel settled and stay in one place for a while. My abundant free time gave Slygore ample opportunity to talk to me. I tried hard to shut him out, but he always had something disruptive to whisper in my ear. The words *you suck* always ended his tirades.

While out for a walk one day, I found a cute little local bookstore about a mile from our apartment. The exterior of the stand-alone building was made of brick and wood with an old-world charm. Inside, the decor was trendy and modern, and a bustling coffee shop was housed inside. I didn't love the taste of coffee at the time, but oddly, I thoroughly enjoyed the smell of it. I'd often spend hours there in the comfy reading chairs, flipping through one book and another. I'd buy an occasional, inexpensive book so the employees didn't think I was simply using the store as my personal library—which I was.

One gloomy Saturday, I entered the store and made my way to my favorite chair, which was tucked away in the back corner. I found a research paper that someone had left behind lying across the seat. I looked around to see if I could find its author, but no one else was nearby. It was almost as though the paper was deliberately left there for me. The information was on human personality patterns. The person who wrote it received an "A" from their professor. I was intrigued, so I gave it a read.

The author was looking at personality differences in ways that made it easy to understand what's going on with other people, as well as themselves. Essentially, the paper explained that much of the pain we carry isn't because of what's happening now—it is created by old safety strategies that helped us survive our childhood traumas but became stuck in our bodies. They've become second nature over time, shaping how we show up in the world, often without our awareness.

The Universe must have left that paper for me because I now knew I needed to understand these personality patterns and how pain gets stuck in the body. I searched around the store for some books on the topic. I ended up in the self-help section. I thought, *Where has this been all my life? An entire part of a bookstore just for me?* I spent the rest of the afternoon scanning several books for any piece of knowledge that might help me make sense of who I was.

Slygore's voice popped into my head several times as I read about emotional maturity, trauma, energy, and other theories regarding the self. He hissed, *Put down the books! None of this will help you. You're broken, unlovable, and you suck.* To his shock, I ignored him and kept reading.

Although, once again, I had no idea how to apply any of the information I learned that day, I left with a few practical books and a sense of hope. A hope that I wasn't the unfixable kind of broken. I was more like a thrift store lamp—slightly wobbly, missing a shade, and questionably wired. I didn't think I was showroom quality, but I also wasn't ready for the landfill either.

Interestingly, about ten years ago or so, my therapist recommended a book by Steven Kessler titled *The Five Personality Patterns*. Reading this book was like rediscovering a lost treasure. Kessler explains that our patterns have shaped us so deeply that now we think that's who we are. But the patterns are not our true selves. They actually cover them up and keep us from shining out in the world. The book provides a straightforward, clear, and relatable map that explains why people behave the way they do and how you can interact with them effectively. The book is brilliant, and it is on the required reading list for all of the staff and program participants at Girls Rise and Shine.

Often, what was kept in the dark, such as my feelings of unworthiness, lack of self-love, and my codependency on others—all things I refused to see at the time—were driving most of my decisions in life. I hoped that I wasn't a completely damaged person, but I was also simultaneously unaware of just how afraid I was of being truly me. I didn't realize that fear was keeping me in the same unwanted patterns of thought and behavior. Even with the discovery of personality patterns and the self-help section of the bookstore, I wasn't at a place in my life where I could do anything with the knowledge. It was as if someone handed me a flashlight when it was dark outside, but the batteries were missing. The flashlight was useless.

I was so used to living in the shadow side of myself that the idea of taking full ownership of my life wasn't even in my awareness—at least not yet. It's strange, right? I had finally reached a point where I wanted to slow down. I was tired of the chaos, the constant overdrive, and the hustle that kept me wired for so long. And now that I was trying to create space for rest and ease, it didn't feel peaceful. It felt . . . uncomfortable, almost like something was missing.

So, instead of looking inward, I redirected the discomfort outward. I needed something to pin it on. So I told myself the problem was Brian and his relentless devotion to his work. The truth is, I didn't know how to live without chaos, so I needed to create more of it. I needed to become the unpredictable one again. This was a pattern in my life I hadn't yet recognized.

It was easier to point at Brian's ambition than to face the parts of me I hadn't even begun to understand. *That must be why the marriage wasn't working for me*, I thought. *If we didn't move so much for Brian's job, things would be easier. He's never around. All he cares about is his career. He doesn't really love me. Maybe if we had a child, he'd love me more, and we could stop moving so much. If I had a child, I would then have unconditional love. But, wait, I can't have children. UGH, I do suck. Slygore's right. Maybe it's time I go see a doctor just to confirm?*

One afternoon, on one of Brian's rare days off, we took a walk on the shores of Lake Washington. After a few minutes, the pressure building inside me had to be released, and I hesitantly said, "Brian, I have something to ask you."

"Sure. What is it?"

"What would you think about trying to have a baby? I mean, I'm not sure I can even have one, but what about the idea of having a baby?"

He stopped and then turned to look at me with his eyebrows raised. "What? Where's this coming from? You've never talked about wanting kids before."

"I know, but I guess I feel like my biological clock is ticking, and if you're willing, I'd like to try. If we can't get pregnant, I'll make an appointment with a specialist. It will all be fine."

"Sure, Julie. I never thought much about wanting to be a dad, but if that's what you want, let's do it. You've given up so much for me over the years, and I know it's been hard on you. I know I'm not home as much as you might like. I really do love you and want you to be happy. If having a baby will make you happy, I'm willing to be a dad!" He hugged me tight and then spun me around. We almost fell into a laughing heap on the waterfront trail.

Though Brian didn't want kids as much as David did, he was willing to be a dad. I realize that just being willing to be a father probably wasn't the best way to approach parenthood, but at the time, I didn't really care. It was nice feeling happy in that moment with him.

For a few months, we tried—and failed—to get pregnant. My nagging fear of being unable to conceive was becoming a constant reminder, which then made me think of David and how I used my infertility as an excuse to end things with him.

Those thoughts, on top of not getting pregnant with Brian, made me feel like a terrible human being. I also couldn't help but worry that Brian would soon leave me once it was confirmed that I was unable to have children. This is why I also avoided going to my OBGYN for so long; I didn't want the confirmation. But ultimately, I needed to put my fears to rest or confirm them, and I knew it was time to seek a medical opinion. So I made the appointment.

A few weeks later, and a long six months after trying to conceive naturally, we visited my OBGYN. Unease felt like a jarring vibration under my skin, and my heart raced. When I was younger, my gynecologists dismissed my concerns and questions as youthful anxiety. They'd say, "You'll get pregnant when it's time." Or "You're too young to worry about that now." I felt like their responses indicated that they didn't hear me and that my concerns were invalid. It always made me angry.

Brian's hands, warm and solid, held mine as the diagnosis came: Endometriosis, stage four, to be exact. My doctor went on to describe my condition in great detail as I mentally zoned out. I'd known from a young age that I couldn't have children. I know that sounds weird, but it's true. The doctor's diagnosis was the confirmation I had dreaded for years. Endometriosis was a clinical term for the deep, personal failure of my own body. *I am indeed broken*, I thought to myself.

As the doctor rambled on, I caught her final suggestions. In vitro fertilization with intracytoplasmic sperm injection, also known as IVF + ICSI. This clinical process became our only potential option for having a biological child.

Looking back, I can see the confusion in it all. I wasn't sure if I had a genuine desire or if having a child was a desperate attempt to fill the voids left by my childhood. Maybe I was trying to prove that I could be of value to someone? Or maybe I was looking for unconditional love? I wish I had considered getting a dog instead. It would have been a better choice!

I expected the doctor to tell me that adoption was our only choice. I didn't fully grasp what the process would be like when we agreed to do the in vitro. It was intense and uncomfortable, to say the least.

Once we began, my body was no longer my own. For months, I lived with the daily invasion of needles, endless fertility drugs, and routine hormone injections. My body became a site for constant clinical examination and evaluation. My eggs and Brian's sperm were reduced to numbers and measurements in Petri dishes. The whole process felt cold and uncomfortable.

I was grateful when the doctor told us we had multiple viable embryos to "work with." Through some miracle, Brian and I had four embryos to implant and three to freeze. Nothing says modern romance like having a bunch of frozen embryos waiting to be defrosted and implanted. I felt like I was running a weird little fertility-themed Dairy Queen. "Welcome to IVF. Would you like one baby or two? Would you like sprinkles or lifelong anxiety with that?" It was an odd experience, that's for sure.

On the day of my scheduled embryo implantation, the doctor said to Brian, "Did you know the uterus is like an English muffin? It's filled with all sorts of nooks and crannies. The embryos must be like the butter so they can settle into one of the deep crevices of the English muffin." Brian said he laughed but thought the guy was a bit strange for sharing that metaphor. I'm sure the doctor was just trying to keep Brain at ease while I was unconscious with my vagina on display. I still can't believe Brian agreed to be in the room for the procedure.

After coming home from the implantation, I was required to lie around and stay as still as possible for twenty-four hours. As I lay in my bed, I thought of my English muffin uterus and tried to will the embryos to settle into a comfortable nesting spot. We had to wait ten very long days before taking a pregnancy test. The wait felt like a bizarre, dreamlike limbo between new hope and a familiar fear.

Apparently, my English muffin was not ready. We had spent over twenty thousand dollars—money we borrowed from credit cards—and all we had to show for it was a negative pregnancy test. It was heartbreaking for both of us. Almost immediately after seeing the single pink line on the little white stick, I visualized Brian walking away from our marriage and me. Slygore added his opinion, *You're a failure. You're broken. And you don't deserve a child. You suck. Go eat worms.* The weight of my inadequacy was almost unbearable.

In a grim twist of timing, nine months later, we tried IVF again with our frozen embryos. For the second time, I endured injections, drugs, and hormones, all with a false optimism and a plastic smile. I was mentally and physically overwhelmed and over the entire process of having a baby. We implanted, we waited, we tested. And again, the results were negative. My slip-n-slide uterus was void of the typical cracks and crevices necessary for a secure implantation of an embryo. I was yet again toppled by another wave of devastating disappointment and tried hard to keep myself from drowning. *Damn you, slippery uterus!*

By this point, we had spent over forty thousand dollars on two failed attempts to conceive a child. Brian was numb and distant. I could tell he was feeling emotional, but he managed to hold it in. It had been almost a year since he agreed to the whole baby plan, and by now, he'd pretty much warmed up to the idea of becoming a dad. But for me, my once-burning desire to bear a child was now quickly fading, and my barren, feminine body felt more useless and vacant than ever.

Within days, Brian began to research other options for us, like surrogacy and adoption, but I desperately needed a break from anything related to a baby. Neither of us was truly mourning the loss we were experiencing. I don't think we knew how. And back then, we weren't assigned a counselor or therapist to help us work through the trauma. Instead of feeling our emotions, we both redirected that energy towards something that we could perceive as controllable. My focus turned to my career, or lack thereof, and Brian buried himself in the chaos of the restaurant.

Shortly after beginning a new job search, I found and accepted a position with a start-up tech company based in Seattle. It was a good fit, and I eventually worked there until I retired. My role in the new company allowed me to work from home, which meant when Brian and I had to move again for his job, I wouldn't have to give up mine. As I began to find my rhythm at work, Brian, ever dedicated to his career, eventually decided to put the baby inquiries on hold.

One afternoon, Brian said, "I hate to say this, Julie, but not getting pregnant was probably for the best. I am busier than ever, and now you have this amazing job that you love. When the time is right, we can revisit the baby situation again. For now, we will just have to wait. I need a break from all this, and

I bet you do too." With a heavy, exhausted tone, he added, "I love you."

"Okay. I love you, too." That was the only response I could muster. I had no argument or counterpoint to his truth in that moment.

As the months passed, I told myself I'd let it go, but in reality, the longing for a child never really left. It stayed tucked in the background. I knew I couldn't physically have my own biological child, but that didn't stop my body from craving the experience. The urge was difficult to ignore.

A friend I had recently met invited me to attend church with her and her family one day. At the time, I had never been a religious or spiritual person, yet somehow, I found myself accepting her random invitation. The church was less "churchy" than most churches I'd attended. This one drew a younger, more modern crowd. I actually liked the pastor and the people. I found the church to be comforting. Since Brian usually worked on Sundays, it made it easier to start attending regular, weekly services with my new friend.

Almost to the day, nine months after the second failed IVF attempt, we were at a potluck lunch after Sunday church service. I met a woman named Jocelyn, a mother with a family of seven kids. She and her husband had three biological children and four adopted, each with special needs. Without knowing anything about me or my IVF failures, Jocelyn began telling me that she and her husband worked with another church to arrange out-of-country adoptions. She told me about a little Ukrainian boy who had just been abandoned at three days old because of a cleft lip and palate. My heart sank.

It felt like a cruel joke that every nine months, an opportunity for a child arrived at my doorstep. Optimistically,

I thought, *Maybe this is my path to becoming a mother.* That afternoon, after Brian came home from work, I told him about the little boy. With exhaustion on his face, he said, "Julie, I thought we put this on pause. We said we were going to wait."

"This isn't a coincidence. He's three days old, Brian. I never gave much thought to adoption, but maybe this is our opportunity?"

"Julie, we just shelled out forty thousand dollars. How much more are we going to spend trying to have a child? And think of all the adoption red tape. We talked about saving for another round of IVF. Don't you want to try that again?"

The thought of more needles and more hormones made my skin crawl. "No. I can't do it. Brian. No more IVF. My body can't go through that again." My words blurted out before I could censor them.

I was terrified of Brian's response. I turned to leave the room before he had a chance to digest what I had just told him. I felt my body grow hot, and a massive surge of energy rushed to my arms and legs. I was angry. I mean, really angry. It felt like all the emotions that I was carrying wanted to just leap out of my body. I needed to get out of the apartment, so I grabbed the car keys and raced toward the door, intentionally digging the keys into my palm.

Slygore's voice snarled in my ear, *He'll leave you now. Drive and don't come back. Leaving him gives you control. Pack up your stuff while Brian is at work tomorrow. Make the first move. Don't let him leave you.* As I hurried to my car, my brain became a tangle of old tapes, all of which replayed the familiar fear of abandonment.

You see, I left David because I was convinced he'd leave me when he realized I wasn't able to bear children. To me, that meant I was damaged goods, unworthy. If he saw me that way, how could he love me? If he no longer loved me, he'd leave me. So, I created any excuse I could to make it easier for *me* to leave first before any of that even happened. Now, here I was again, trapped in the same irrational logic. But it wasn't actually logic; it was neurology.

Neurology, at its core, is the story of how our brains turn experience into memory and memory into maps—internal blueprints that help us navigate the world. The problem is that those maps aren't usually updated. Sometimes, the brain marks a place as dangerous because it was—not because it still is. So, even long after the threat is gone, the signal remains. A look, a sound, or a smell can light up an old alarm like it's happening all over again.

My brain couldn't tell the difference between then and now. I had lost the ability to separate my experiences with Susan, David, and Brian. I had no way of knowing if what I said to Brian fell into the category of "Things Julie says or does to make people leave her."

Later that night, after the adrenaline ran its course, I returned home, bracing for a fight and preparing for the end. But Brian had a kind and steady heart and just wanted to understand me and what I needed. He wanted me to be happy. While I was driving like a mad woman, he had taken time to emotionally and rationally think about us adopting a child. He was willing to explore the idea and wanted to know more about the little boy from Ukraine. I envied that calm, sensible side of Brian. That was a skill set I had yet to master.

To understand what we were getting into, we met with the church, the local organization that helped facilitate the adoption, a Ukrainian adoption organization, a pediatrician, and Jocelyn and her husband. We then spoke with a coordinator who explained the whole European adoption process and a financial counselor. It felt like the exhaustive and sterile process of IVF all over again. We faced numerous policies, endless paperwork, and way too many hoops to jump through, all for the chance to adopt this little boy. It wasn't until we saw his beautiful, angelic face and his wispy, dark brown hair that we knew he was our child. It was love at first sight.

The adoption process was the labyrinth of paperwork we expected and then some. Once all of the i's were dotted and t's were crossed, we were told we just needed to wait. So we waited. And while we waited, we named him Antin—a Ukrainian name meaning worthy of praise. We sent money abroad for his private care and for surgery to repair his cleft lip and palate.

As the weeks and months went by, we waited and watched grainy videos of him playing and living his everyday life in Ukraine. We put together a nursery at home and painted the walls a soft, uplifting yellow. Even though he wasn't yet legally or physically our child, emotionally, he was already part of our lives. Our family and friends even threw a baby shower for us. We couldn't wait to meet him in person and begin our lives as a family.

After nearly a year of waiting for the adoption to become final, we got a devastating phone call instead. Our US adoption agency explained a crippling new change in the Ukrainian adoption law. All adoptions were suspended until further notice, including those already in progress, which meant our adoption was suspended, too.

They used the word suspended at the time, but I found out several years later that the Ukrainian government decided to close all adoptions to foreigners indefinitely. Unless you were a citizen of Ukraine, you could no longer adopt from that country. I can only imagine how many other families and children were affected by this decision. Even now, I often think about our little boy and who he became in this world. I wonder what he looks like. Does he have a family of his own now? Is he happy, healthy, and safe? I try not to let myself go down that path too much; the heartache is still there.

We spent eleven months building a life around a child we'd not yet held or touched. We spent eleven months deeply loving and opening our hearts to a child we'd seen only in videos and photos. To us, Antin was already a part of our family. He was our little boy; we just hadn't met yet.

After we hung up the phone, I turned to Brian in shock. "Surely this can't be happening. He is our child, right? Tell me this isn't happening, Brian. What is going on? Why can't we have a child? What did I do so wrong in my life to deserve this? You don't deserve this. What do we do now?" I was half shouting, half crying, and grabbing both sides of my head in a futile effort to stop my mind from spinning.

"Not anymore," he replied, his voice flat. I didn't hear the same anguish from him that I was experiencing. I needed a hug and wanted to embrace him, but I couldn't. I felt like I had failed Brian again, and my body wouldn't let me feel any kind of connection with him at that moment. I was physically frozen.

We sat separately in the heavy silence of Antin's empty nursery that night. The loss and the pain were real, nearly unbearable, even more so than the failed IVFs. I didn't allow myself to look at the pain on Brian's face, nor did I ask him how he was feeling about the loss of our little boy. I was too consumed with myself. I was solely wrapped up in believing that I had caused yet another failure. That I was the problem.

That I had given Brian one more reason to leave me. For days, I disregarded him as much as I disregarded myself. It was so much easier than allowing myself to feel and to grieve yet another loss.

Brian and I spent nearly all of our fiscal and emotional capital attempting to bring a child into our lives. We were in debt, childless, and completely disconnected from one another. To make matters worse, within two weeks of learning our adoption had been suspended, Brian's sister, a woman who had always declared her aversion to children, announced she was pregnant. The news felt like a cruel twist aimed directly at Brian and me.

I took it very personally. I remember angrily shouting at Brian, "Your sister doesn't even want kids. What a fucking joke!" He said nothing.

For months, my sadness, shame, and guilt twisted themselves into something darker—self-hatred. I wanted to run, to isolate myself from everyone, but I didn't have the strength at the time. Instead, I turned my pain inward. I needed to be angry at someone, so I chose myself. I wandered down the familiar roads of self-pity and self-punishment. Deep down, I think I needed people to be angry with me too—just enough to confirm what I already feared, that I wasn't worthy of love in the first place. Slygore was in his glory. His nasty chattering was like one of those kitschy songs you'd hear that you can't get out of your head, no matter how hard you tried.

About three months after our adoption plan went up in smoke, I told Brian that I wanted a divorce. I was done with our marriage. Done with adoption. Done with all of it. I hated who I was and who he knew me to be. I didn't stop to think or even care about what Brian wanted, let alone needed or felt. I couldn't handle my own emotions and feelings; no way in hell could I hold space for Brian.

I felt like a horrible person on the inside, yet I still wore the stoic smile on the outside.

My marriage to Brian ended when I was thirty-four years old. It ended, in part, because that version of me was operating from outdated, deep-seated patterns. That version of me believed herself to be broken, damaged, and unlovable and made decisions from a place of lack rather than a place of wholeness. It also ended because it all wore me down. I exhausted myself emotionally. I burned through every fight, every silent treatment, every attempt to make him the problem. I was tired from the performance. And when I couldn't keep it up anymore, I did what seemed like the only option left; I gave up and asked Brian for a divorce. I was too worn out to keep pretending I was okay. I didn't know how to fix what was broken in me, and I couldn't face the emptiness I felt in the absence of chaos.

What hurt me the most was not the end of the marriage itself but the sinking feeling that I had been the one to sabotage it, and I didn't even fully understand why. Brian saw something in me I didn't see in myself, and I tried to make that enough. But love given freely isn't the same as love returned—and I never really truly met his eyes in the mirror.

As I returned to the present, I looked almost shyly at Laura and asked, "Are you noticing the irony here with regard to Susan?"

"Yes. Is this what you call an inherited generational wound? From Susan, and possibly even her mother, too? Throughout my career, I've interviewed hundreds of women, and I've learned a great deal about unconscious, inherited cycles.

Daughters often internalize their mothers' unprocessed emotions—grief, anger, shame—and unknowingly repeat them. Is that what you're talking about?"

"Yes, exactly. Some of the stories I carried were inherited, and some were born of experience. Just like Susan, I created chaos, pushed love away, and walked out when things got too quiet—too close. I was, unknowingly, following Susan's same script. Different scenery, different cast, but it was the same emotional blueprint."

Laura leaned back in her seat, letting silence settle before responding. Then she said, "I'm starting to clearly understand why the work you do within your organization has such a powerful effect on so many people. It's undoubtedly very personal to you. You aren't just influencing the current generation of women. You're helping them break generational cycles—past, current, and future."

"Yes, and we've been able to see that already with many of the women. Breaking these cycles is key because they will continue until they're seen. Seeing the patterns is where healing begins, not in blame but in awareness. We weren't born with self-doubt, exhaustion, or the need to constantly prove our worth. Somewhere along the way, we learned to adapt, survive, and keep going—often at the cost of our health, peace, and true self."

I paused for a moment to gather my thoughts before continuing. "As the women move through our programs, they begin to reflect on the wounds they've inherited, and they're also empowered to choose something new for themselves. Once the cycle is seen, it can finally be interrupted. And that's when something incredible becomes possible, the choice to live as their true self rather than as a continuation of inherited pain. That's true liberation."

I smirked slightly, raised an eyebrow, and added, "That kind of liberation took me many years and numerous therapists to consciously achieve. All of my patterns, beliefs, and behaviors continued to be present in my next, and third, marriage with Andy, too. It was as if I was an express train with no stops. I just barreled through life, full speed ahead, with no time to slow down and no interest in looking out the window until I crashed.

"You see, I didn't get divorced twice because I didn't want love—I left David and Brian because I didn't know how to receive it without losing myself in the process. By the time I married Andy, whom I'll tell you about next, I had unconsciously adopted a very different strategy. A strategy that was far more stoic and emotionally detached, almost businesslike in nature.

"Today, I can and do appreciate the experiences I had with Brian. I may not have loved him the way I wish I could have or in the ways that he deserved, but I can't apologize for who I was when I knew him. He was a part of my path and the lessons I needed to learn in this lifetime—lessons that helped shape me into who I am today. And I have tremendous gratitude for that part of my life."

EIGHT

I paused, stretched, and said, "Laura, if you don't need a break or anything, I can dive right into my life with Andy."

I could hear the light rain tapping at the window and didn't want to disturb Lily, if at all possible. Lily loved playing in the rain, a good quality for a dog living in Washington, and I knew Lily would want to go out to pee if she woke up. I didn't want to deal with drying off a wet and muddy dog at the moment, as I knew Laura had a plane to catch in the evening and still needed to hear about Andy and Todd and how all of this added up to where my life is today.

"I'm good. We can just continue. But I'd love another cup of coffee if you can manage to get it without disturbing Lily. She looks so sweet when she is sleeping."

Lily let out a snore so loud it startled her own ears—she lifted her head, blinked once, and then flopped back down like nothing had happened. Laura and I laughed without making a sound.

Carefully, I got up, picked up the carafe, and refilled Laura's coffee. "Thank you," Laura whispered.

I refreshed my cup, too, and then quietly eased back into my chair, ready to continue.

Twice divorced. Twice failed. I couldn't bear to face or dissect the tangled mess of my emotions after my divorce from Brian, so I did what I always did. I buried them. Out of sight, out of mind. This was my childish counter-approach to internal chaos.

The flexibility I had at my company allowed me to work from home, so I decided to pack up my life once again and move to Westport, Washington. It's a small coastal town about two hours west of Des Moines. I was craving the familiarity of reinvention. And I was good at it. I rented a cute little apartment right in the middle of town, even though I didn't know a single soul there. I can't remember how or why I picked that quiet coastal city, but it offered me another blank slate— new routines, new scenery, and a new identity.

As I've mentioned, my physical body was rarely happy with stillness. It demanded movement. It demanded to express and release its pent-up emotions, especially all of the subconscious guilt I was carrying by that point in my life. I had no viable outlet for my emotions. All that bottled-up stuff was creating a weird, unconscious need to punish myself—like it was the only way to let out the pain.

So, I joined Bigfoot Surf School. Now, you might be thinking that's a bit odd for someone in her early thirties who has no surfing experience whatsoever. And I guess, in retrospect, it was odd.

I sometimes never understood the rhyme or reason for the impulsive and random decisions I made. I just went with them, trusting some inner part of me knew my path.

The outside of the surf school building was old and rusty from the salt air and was oddly located at the edge of a huge parking lot. It looked like someone had taken a colorful backyard shed and just plopped it down in a space meant for a parked car.

When I joined the surf school, I must have looked like a deer in the headlights. I was unprepared, out of shape, clumsy, and felt like I looked desperate to fit in. It was mainly a "guys" group. Only two other women showed up inconsistently for lessons, and they were significantly younger than I was. Nearly everyone had some kind of surfing experience, and it seemed that everyone knew each other. I was the oldest student and the only true beginner. It was humbling.

The school had three rotating instructors. Each of them embodied equal qualities of a lifeguard, a cheerleader, and a Zen master. Mike looked like he hadn't worn real shoes since 1998 and believed coconut water could cure everything. Jon was the only person I knew who could give a safety lecture while holding a breakfast burrito and still make it sound like gospel. And Barry—who was technically the "head instructor," mostly because he had a whistle and yelled things like "Send it!" even when we were clearly not ready.

Andy wasn't on the surf school student roster. He was friends with Mike and Jon and would often come by to surf and hang out. He was young—ten years younger than me, to be exact. I didn't pay him much attention, but Andy would give me the occasional nod to say hello when he saw me. I could never tell if he acknowledged me because he felt sorry for me or because he was just being polite. I had a way of crashing into the waves, crashing into my own board, and swallowing half the ocean. All this made me look like I was on a suicide mission.

Andy was sexy. His tall, lanky body was perfectly proportioned. His shoulders were broad, his hips were trim, and his limbs carried long, lean muscles. His dark brown hair often drifted across his sparkling green eyes. His skin was a slight olive color and very tan, which was odd for a guy born and raised in the state of Washington and who lived in a wetsuit. Andy was quiet, mostly kept to himself, and had a bashful smile as if he didn't know how handsome he was. I was not looking for a new romance at all, but the more we interacted, the more I couldn't help but become attracted to him.

As I got to know him through our evolving, flirtatious interactions, one of the things I found most alluring was Andy's simplicity. He didn't care much for big crowds and social events. He was comfortable in his small, close-knit circle of friends. He was more of a homebody. He wasn't looking to build a mega-career. He didn't talk about politics or gossip about the other guys on the beach. He didn't want kids and wasn't interested in talking about kids. He just wanted to have fun and live his life day by day. Although he was very introverted, I found him easy to talk to.

Over the following weeks, we began to see each other outside of our beach setting and then started dating casually. Andy, along with his friends Mike and Jon, soon became the bulk of my social life. His circle was a collective mix of guys ranging in age from twenty-four to forty. In addition to Mike and Jon, one guy owned a decent-sized plumbing business in town, another owned a marine welding shop, and one was a teacher. Andy was a backyard boat mechanic.

Several of the guys, including Andy, were training for surf competitions. I had seen these kinds of competitions on TV before, but I never really knew what went into preparing for one. Weeks before the competitions, they were hyper-focused on their physical conditioning, often cross-training with other sports. They prepared their gear as if they were waiting for an apocalypse, thoroughly studied the location and the break of each event location, and routinely reviewed the scoring criteria. It was a whole thing!

I liked hanging out with Andy and the guys and going to the surfing competitions. I learned a great deal by watching them and was able to hone my surfing skills as a result. It was fun. I did, however, feel a bit odd dating someone much younger than me, especially in the company of guys my age. But Andy and I had a mutual spark that neither one of us wanted to deny. On the beach, the age gap didn't matter so much. We spoke the same language—pearling, wipeout, kook, turtle roll.

Off the beach was a different story. Andy seemed anxious. He preferred staying home or coming over to my apartment at night. He wasn't much for going out to the bars or listening to live music in the neighboring towns like the rest of his friends. He avoided most social activities, which I found rather puzzling for someone his age.

Our shared experiences also highlighted the age gap. For example, one evening, we talked about music. Andy declared with a mischievous glint in his eyes, "Nirvana and Red Hot Chili Peppers are the best bands ever!"

I stared at him, incredulous. "Are you serious? Nirvana was a flash in the pan. Depeche Mode and the Cure are way better."

"No way, Curt Cobain is a legend."

"Yeah, a legend who took himself out when he was not much older than you."

The argument, though playful, highlighted a divide. Andy was a teenager of the 1990s with its grunge fashion of flannel shirts and ripped jeans. I had been a teen in a different era, with different cultural memories. This dance between attraction and generational difference was obvious, but the fun, physical connection was just the escape I needed in my life.

As the months passed, I did find myself yearning, at times, for a more mature, adult-like relationship. I craved a deeper, more robust connection like the ones I had with David and Brian. I wanted a relationship that would transcend conversations about rock bands and protein shakes. Deep down, I knew a man in his mid-twenties couldn't fully satisfy my need for an emotionally rich relationship, but I continued to date Andy anyway.

Andy had moved back in with his parents after graduating college, which made visiting him where he lived rather awkward for me. It made me feel small and embarrassed, as if I were a young kid myself. His living at home with his mom reminded me of just how young he was. So, after six months of dating, I asked Andy if he wanted to move in with me. He was twenty-five years old.

I pushed Andy and his mom way out of their comfort zones with that suggestion. Andy was anguished over the decision. I could tell he wanted to, but he was stuck overanalyzing what his parents would think. He also worried about the cost of moving out on his own. He thought he'd need to get a better job and wondered if he was really ready to be away from home. His mom thought it was too soon into our relationship, and she knew I had been married before. That made her nervous. She was cautious and had every right to be.

You might think all that would've been a big red flag for a twice-divorced woman with a lot of life experience, and it was, but I dismissed the thoughts circling in my head. It wasn't until shortly after Andy moved in with me, and I stopped spending so much time surfing with him, that I started to see just how immature our relationship truly was.

Still, I continued ignoring every warning sign that arose. Our relationship was fun. Life together was simple. It was easy. And unknowingly, Andy was allowing me to re-establish a feeling of control. Control I felt I had lost while trying to bring a child into my life.

Not only did I convince Andy to move into my apartment, but a month after he moved in, I took it one step further and got us a puppy. She wasn't just a puppy—she became like the child I never had. In her, I found the kind of bond I imagined I'd one day have with a child—pure, devoted, and healing in ways I never expected. She was a Cane Corso, and we named her Cobain, after Nirvana's lead singer, who Andy idolized. Cobain was an imposing figure. She was loyal and deeply devoted to me. She lived to be twelve years old, which was nearly unheard of for her breed. My heart still flutters when I think of her. I miss that giant girl dearly.

By this time in my life, my career was soaring, and Andy, much to my surprise, landed an entry-level job in construction. Our not-so-little puppy was growing quickly, and I found myself pushing for the next big step—buying a house together.

It was all moving way too quickly for Andy. He didn't have much money to contribute for the down payment, but when I told him I would be covering that part, he agreed. He said he trusted me to make decisions for us, but really, he relied on me to make almost all of them. And no one had ever leaned on me like that before. It felt overwhelming . . . and, oddly enough, kind of fulfilling.

The home we purchased was a two-story, forest-green, three-bedroom house near downtown Westport. It wasn't flashy or new, but it had a big backyard for Cobain. It was just big enough to feel cozy for Andy and me.

Andy now had a full-time job working for GLS Construction and said he felt "grown-up" because he could cover his portion of the monthly mortgage payment. I remember thinking that maybe I had been too hasty in thinking our relationship wasn't mature enough for me. *Andy's becoming more of an adult. This just might work.*

Shortly after we bought the house, Andy began to stay home more often with Cobain and me. He was surfing less and less and wasn't hanging out with Mike and Jon as much. I was now either spending endless hours working, redecorating our house from top to bottom, or navigating the frenzy only a giant puppy can create. My tendency towards control was becoming increasingly prevalent.

I was older, earned significantly more money, had more life experience, and was in the midst of a rapidly developing career. I liked feeling Andy's reliance on me. It made me feel like I had a purpose—like I was needed. At times, I had to remind myself that I wasn't Andy's mom or caretaker. Part of me needed Andy to mature and be my equal partner, and another part of me wanted, or rather needed, him to need me. What I failed to recognize at the time was that I had projected not only my insatiable need to care for a child onto Cobain but also onto Andy.

It wasn't lost on me that, eventually, Andy would want to get married someday. I, however, did not want to get married again. Selfishly, I wanted to continue living together to see if the relationship would actually pan out. Our relationship had many positive aspects, like our shared passion for outdoor sports and other athletic activities, his uncomplicated nature, and his genuinely kind demeanor. We had loads of fun together, which was something I had been missing for much of my life.

When Andy eventually proposed, Athena's voice popped into my head, *Tell him no, Julie. I know you love him, but ask to keep things the way they are. You don't want to be married again. Be kind. Be honest.* But do you think I listened? Nope. Does this sound familiar? Remember the day of my marriage to Brian and how Athena offered the same advice before I walked down the aisle? I didn't listen to her the day I married him, and I didn't listen to her when Andy proposed, either.

How could I deny Andy the opportunity to marry? I'm the one who pushed for us to live together, get a dog, and buy a house together. I thought, *You knew he'd think this was the next logical step in your relationship. What were you expecting? You suck, Julie.* My own thoughts picked up Slygore's grating tone, and I felt slightly sick to my stomach.

As guilt weighed heavily on my heart at that moment, I dismissed my intuition to decline Andy's marriage proposal. My answer came in a quiet "Yes," almost lost in the air. I wanted to make him happy.

After giving Andy my reluctant yes, he wanted to move quickly on the wedding. He was excited and began offering up ideas regarding the location, the date, and potential attendees. He was almost obsessing over it. I, on the other hand, didn't really care how, where, or when we tied the knot. I just wanted it to be small. I actually would've preferred eloping, but since it was Andy's first marriage, he wanted something more substantial.

"Tell you what, let's get married in Las Vegas. Just us," I said one night.

"Vegas? You want to get married in Vegas?"

"Why not? It'll be fun. No fuss, no drama."

"But don't you want a big wedding? And what about my family? What about the guys . . . "

"Andy, it's not about them. It's about us. And honestly? The less people, the better."

He looked at me like I'd spoken in fluent alien. The truth was, the anonymity of Vegas appealed to me. We could have a quick, convenient ceremony amidst a blur of neon and noise. No expectations, no pressure. I think a part of me hoped the old adage would hold true: What happens in Vegas, stays in Vegas.

"Okay," he said finally, his shoulders relaxing. "Okay, Vegas, it is. Just us."

For whatever reason, Andy agreed with me. He didn't mind the idea of fewer people after he gave it some thought. His introverted social anxiety balked at the thought of a big, traditional wedding. He said he only suggested a big wedding because he thought that's what I would want. For him, Las Vegas offered a kind of refuge in its own bizarre way.

Our wedding took place a few months later at the Las Vegas Neon Museum. The place is like a beautiful graveyard of glitz. We were surrounded by the faded glow of what used to be—old casinos, motels, and lounges. The irony here was that we were saying "I do" in front of a lineup of failed romances and bankrupt fantasies. As a surprise to me, Andy had arranged for an Elvis impersonator to perform the ceremony, which added to the strangely poetic environment.

Intellectually, I knew I should have felt joy, pleasure, or excitement. Instead, I drifted through the day and the ceremony with a strange sense of detachment. To me, having done this twice before, this felt more like Andy's day. What mattered was that he was happy.

Athena tried to warn me that morning. *Don't do it, Julie. You're going to regret this. It's not fair to Andy.* Still, I ignored her as I often did.

Married life with Andy was relatively easy. We weren't shuffling from city to city, we weren't worried about having children, and we didn't have much to argue about. Our relationship was devoid of any real chaos or turmoil, resembling the start of a newly cemented daily routine.

And just like in my marriages to David and Brian, the ease and the quiet started to feel uncomfortable. I began needing that familiar buzz of drama. I once again began to operate from old wiring I hadn't yet questioned.

This time, my pattern emerged in the form of cleanliness, order, structure, and rigid daily schedules. Everything in our house had a place. Only certain appliances were to be on the kitchen counter at any given time. Once Cobain's feeding and naptime routines were established, I obsessed over dirt on the floors and even made Andy cut the grass in a particular diagonal design. I think Andy was able to put up with all of my idiosyncrasies, but he was dealing with his own form of social anxiety. He recognized much of himself in me, and my behaviors didn't scare him.

Case in point, Stan and his wife came for a visit. When they arrived after a long day of travel, I immediately made them put their suitcases in the guest room closet; I didn't want their bags cluttering up the house. I made my stepmom use a coaster for her drink by shoving it under her sweating cup after she carelessly placed it on top of the wooden coffee table. My dad plopped down hard enough on our couch that the couch even made a noise. I cringed. But, get this . . . he wasn't even in the middle of the cushions. He was on the edge . . . with his weight pressing into the cushion's side. I mean, how dare someone do that, right?

A flutter started in my chest, and then my heart began to pound. Slygore chanted, *Wrong. Wrong. Wrong. Wrong.*

In a tight, strained voice that tried for a veneer of politeness, I said, "Dad, could you sit in the middle of the cushion, please?"

He heard the quake in my voice and looked up, surprised. "What? What's wrong?"

"The cushion," I said. "You're sitting on the edge of the cushion. You need to sit in the middle. You'll squash it out of shape."

He looked at me with confusion and a touch of concern. Like maybe I was ill or something. My anxiety and need for control crashed over any semblance of reason. Slygore was shouting inside my head, *He's ruining it. He's ruining it! Just like you, your couch is ruined!*

"Dad, you need to move. To the middle of the cushion," I repeated.

With slow, deliberate movements, he shifted his position. His gaze never wavered from my eyes. I paid no attention to the bewilderment they reflected. I could only see an unevenly weighted cushion finally smoothing out.

I should have been relieved that he agreed to shift his weight without questioning me. Instead, I felt shame for treating him that way. Luckily, just then, Andy walked into the room, which offered a welcome distraction.

It's hard not to laugh now as I retell that story. Stan still jokes about it today, finding the whole thing endearing now. Looking back on it, I understand that moment much better. My neglected inner child was screaming for order in a world that still felt fundamentally unsafe. I didn't know those terms then. I just knew the feeling—the unruly energy surging through my veins, the frantic heartbeat, the sense that I was on the verge of implosion. I was much like a live wire threatening to ignite at any moment.

The good news about marrying a much younger guy was that he was always up for something sporty, which, in turn, offered the perfect outlet for my wound-up energy. We typically sought out activities with people we knew or group activities in smaller circles so Andy would feel more comfortable. Meeting new people and hanging out in crowded places still made him feel overwhelmed, and at times, rather shut down.

Luckily for us both, the sport of cycling entered the picture. Andy and I decided we wanted to explore the world of mountain biking. Andy was a natural. Me, not so much. He gracefully rode the dirt trails with ease. I don't recall him even falling once. I struggled with the clip-in pedals, and I think I managed to scrape, bruise, or cut nearly every part of my legs and arms on the first few rides.

We both loved being outdoors and feeling that adrenaline rush that accompanied flying down steep ravines, around sharp corners, and dodging tall, thick pine trees. We had so much fun that we ended up buying new bikes from the local bike shop. After a few more weekends of riding and repeatedly bringing my crash-prone bike back to the shop for repairs, we slowly started to form a budding friendship with the owner and his wife.

As our skills developed and the friendship with the shop owners bloomed, they introduced Andy and me to the sport of road cycling, local group rides, and regional amateur races. Months later, after Andy's comfort zone expanded and we got to know some of the people, we were both invited to join their shop's amateur cycling team. Road cycling became a sport Andy and I could enjoy together. Everyone on the team was friendly, and it was much easier getting to know people while riding down a country road than on a rugged mountain trail.

Ultimately, we both took up the thrilling discipline of cyclocross. Cyclocross is what happens when someone looks at a perfectly good bike ride and says, "You know what this needs? Mud, stairs, and the occasional need to carry your bike like a wounded comrade through a war zone."

It's part road cycling, part steeplechase, and part slip 'n slide, held on short, loopy courses packed with grass, gravel, sand pits, and barriers explicitly designed to ruin your momentum. Riders dismount mid-race to hurdle obstacles, climb hills, or run through mud puddles like it's a two-wheeled boot camp.

Races last about an hour—but there was more than enough time to question my life choices while sliding sideways through a muddy corner, face covered in dirt, heart pounding like a techno remix. And did I mention the races are usually held in fall and winter? Nothing says fun like freezing rain, snow, and numb fingers.

In short, cyclocross is for people who think traditional biking isn't chaotic enough. The races were raw, brutal, and exhausting, and I loved every minute of it.

After five years of racing cyclocross, the pinnacle moment arrived when I won the most demanding race on that year's circuit on my thirty-ninth birthday. It was a beautiful reward for my previous years of dedication to the sport and a great birthday present.

I surprised myself when I quit the team and the entire sport shortly after. Andy kept racing for the team, but I was done with cycling after winning that race. I didn't quit cycling because I wasn't good at it. I was good. I was better than I expected. That wasn't the problem. Once the sport stopped feeling like a scramble for survival and started feeling stable, I got scared. I told myself I simply lost interest.

Sound familiar? Cyclocross, much like David, Brian, and Andy, served as both an outlet and mirror for my unresolved emotional wiring. If only I had known.

Something in me changed after that birthday. I was finally able to admit to myself that my marriage to Andy was unfulfilling. I needed more. Here we go again, I thought to myself. What in the hell is wrong with me? I am seriously demented. Then Slygore echoed with a sneering set of words that were all too familiar, *You suck!*

In true form, I stuffed my unwanted thoughts and feelings away, much like I had done in my past relationships. I had done this for months, hoping that this time, the outcome would be different. It wasn't.

So, I took an interest in other sports—rock climbing, running, yoga—to redirect the emotional energy that had now returned to my body. Andy tried all of those activities with me for a while, but he didn't love them as much as cycling. I discovered that I loved the feeling of freedom that running gave me and set my sights on training for the local Run Like the Wind Half Marathon.

Training for the half marathon was intense and time-consuming. Andy was left tending to Cobain most nights and weekends and missed spending time with me. I missed being home, too, but running allowed me to move. It gave my guilt, my shame, and my grief somewhere to go. Guilt from failed relationships. Shame from who I had become. Grief over my barren womb. I wasn't actually running to anything. I was running from everything. I was basically in my Forrest Gump era—minus the beard and the accidental cult following.

As the day of the half marathon approached and my training was coming to an end, Andy asked me if I'd be interested in learning to play tennis with him. He was on the tennis team in both high school and college and missed playing. He said it was something we could do together again, just like when we used to cycle. He suggested I would like it and it would be fun for us both. I appreciated Andy's eagerness to find a new connection with me. He really was a sweet guy. Too sweet, in fact.

I completed the scenic route in just under one hour and fifty-five minutes. My goal time was two hours. I was happily shocked. Andy joyously greeted me at the finish line. I kissed him quickly, then graciously accepted the race medal and the foil blanket. My legs felt like they were made of concrete and overcooked spaghetti combined. After catching my breath and taking inventory of my aches and pains, I noticed I had lost sight of Andy, so I found a spot on the curb of the road where I collapsed from exhaustion. I took my time eating the banana and drinking the Gatorade the race staff gave me.

My entire body felt like it had just gotten off a hamster wheel—literally and physically. It had been spinning fast enough for months, years even, to avoid the fact that I was failing in my marriage to Andy. Sitting on that curb was the first time I permitted myself to admit that I no longer wanted to be married to him.

The deep sense of needing to end my relationship overshadowed any happiness from my well-deserved running accomplishment. And in a celebratory hiss, Slygore chanted at me like the mean kid on the playground, *You're no good at relationships. You're a loser. Nobody loves you. You should go eat worms.*

I didn't even try to call Andy on his cell to see where he was. I wanted to be alone. I dragged myself up off the curb, and with mixed emotions and in a daze, I made the trek back to my car, wobbly legs and all. I bitterly thought, What the hell is wrong with me? Why am I not overjoyed with what I just accomplished? I trained for months and should be happy right now.

Athena tried to soothe me with, *You'll be okay. Just breathe.* Though I found small comfort in her words, I knew deep down that I was just drifting through my life. She then said to me, *You know this isn't going to fill the hole, right?* She was being honest with me, as she always was, but this time, I heard her—at least a little. She wanted me to know that no amount of gold stars or applause could fix the part of me that still believed I wasn't enough. She was right, but I didn't fully let her words land.

I should've been an expert at ending marriages by now, but this one was different. With David and Brian, I had a perceived, albeit contrived, reason for leaving those relationships, both of which centered around my inability to have a child. That wasn't the case with Andy. There was no infertility heartbreak to rally behind. I felt unmoored, as if the ground beneath me had just shifted. I had no "real" reason for leaving other than my own lack of fulfillment. I had nothing to blame for my disconnection with him or our marriage.

Andy had felt like my responsibility for most of our relationship, so the idea of leaving him and our marriage felt incredibly heavy. It added a layer of guilt I wasn't expecting. So many thoughts circled in my mind. *I took Andy from his mother's home. I generated the majority of our household's income. I made all of the big decisions. Where would he go now? Would leaving him make his anxiety worse? What about Cobain? I can't leave her.*

When I finally reached my car, I was drained. I opened the door and plopped down in the driver's seat. I grabbed my post-race meal from my little cooler, and as I took the first bite, tears streamed down my face. I felt like a hot mess, and I knew this wasn't the time to make big life decisions. I also knew that people don't just walk away from marriages because they're unfulfilled. *Or do they? Do I really need something concrete and justifiable? Maybe it would be okay to simply walk away, right?* Without clear answers, leaving Andy would have to wait.

In the weeks and months following the race, life blurred into a routine of pretending. I pretended to be happy and hid behind my smile. I built a version of happiness I didn't feel. Andy received a promotion at work and began working out at the gym more often. He seemed content and a little more confident in his skin. I devoted more of my time and energy to my career and Cobain, and also kept my promise to Andy about tennis.

A few of the neighborhood parks had tennis courts, and after work and on weekends, Andy started teaching me how to play. He was right; he was good at the game and a good teacher, and I liked it. I picked up the sport fairly quickly, and within a few months, we were playing full matches with one another. Andy always beat me, of course, but he made it seem like he had to work for the win. He was kind like that. I hated myself for feeling so emotionally distant from him.

After one of our evening matches, Andy told me that while he was cheering me on during the half-marathon, he felt overwhelmed by the crowds and the noise. He felt anxious and trapped, more so than usual in big crowds. At one point, he said he felt frozen and that his heart was beating out of his chest. He admitted leaving me in the crowd of people after the race because he felt ashamed and needed to get home. He went on to tell me that the experience prompted him to see a therapist, who then recommended him to a psychiatrist specializing in social anxiety disorders.

"Wow, Andy. I'm proud of you. That takes a lot of self-awareness to admit you need help. I'm sure that wasn't an easy thing to do. When did you do this?" I asked him as I gently rubbed his hand.

"About a month ago. I didn't want to tell you right away. I wanted to understand my diagnosis better. My psychotherapist thinks I have high-functioning autism. She said I've been able to mask it well because I've learned specific coping strategies. It's not what I was expecting, but it does answer a lot of questions I have about myself. Oh, and they issued me some medication to help with my symptoms while we use what she called evidence-based approaches. She wants me to start group therapy."

I was genuinely impressed. Here he was—with an actual diagnosis, a decade younger than me, and with way less life experience under his belt—getting his shit together. I was proud of him. I was also jealous. Andy could admit to himself that he needed help working through his thoughts, his behaviors, and his fears. Yet here I was, like some self-absorbed child, still running away from all my problems.

Then I heard Slygore's voice. *When he starts getting this under control, he's gonna realize that he doesn't love you. He just can't see it yet. He's gonna leave you. You suck!*

After listening to Andy share vulnerably what he had learned about himself, I should've been more loving, more comforting, and more supportive, but I couldn't. Slygore was right. That's been the issue all along. I told myself I couldn't connect with Andy in any meaningful way because of his anxiety, that it held him back from building genuine connections. Yet, I could feel the brittleness of the lie.

Slygore soothed me away from my awareness of my false thinking, *Yes, that's it. His anxiety issues created the problem in your marriage.* I clung to this flimsy and false excuse like a life preserver. *Ah, this is why you are unhappy, Julie.* Needless to say, this became the reason I needed to end my marriage to Andy.

Within six months, I told Andy I was done with our marriage. I was done with him, and I wanted a divorce. I should've just had business cards made with those words printed on them. That's how often I felt like I said the phrase. He pleaded with me to reconsider. He didn't want to lose me or the life we'd built. He didn't want to lose Cobain either. He knew I would take her with me. He was devastated.

The weight of the guilt I felt pressed on my chest like a cinder block. Reluctantly, I even agreed to stay for a few more months while he worked more intensely with his therapist. I told him I'd give us time. But it was a lie. By this time, I had already checked out. Emotionally. Physically. I was there, but I wasn't with him. And I crossed lines I couldn't uncross. I'm not proud of it, but at the time, staying a few months felt easier than facing the truth of another divorce.

I was a master of denial and deflection. I refused to see my own outdated survival patterns and my role in the disintegration of this marriage. Like I did with the others, it was easier to blame Andy than to believe I was the problem. I did everything possible to ignore the inconvenient truth that I was running again—running from myself, from my unresolved pain.

Andy was much braver than I was at the time, and I'm not proud of betraying Andy the way that I did. I was a coward.

From the inception of my relationship with Andy, I felt out of control on the inside. I was embarrassed about who I had become. I thought people could see the unworthiness in me and knew I was a fraud. I believed they silently judged and pitied me. And except for my rather noticeable control issues, I don't think most people knew of my insecurities and depression. I had learned to hide those things well.

Andy's struggles were a mirror, reflecting my hidden wounds back to me. I just wouldn't allow myself to look. During those years, the protective parts of me helped me hide from nearly everyone in my life—everyone except him.

The Universe brilliantly aligns us with those who mirror back to us the aspects we need to heal. If we're lucky and have created a positive self-worth, they can also reflect this back to us. It took me many more years before I would move into a place of self-love and self-worth.

The problems in our marriage weren't Andy's fault at all. I think I knew that all along. The issue wasn't the age gap, his anxieties, or even my insatiable need for control. It was about the gaping hole inside of me that I tried to fill with yet another person, another relationship, another fleeting illusion of wholeness.

But when we divorced, I still didn't know any of this. And even though I was the common denominator in all of my, now three, divorces, I still couldn't see myself. I wasn't ready—yet.

I was grateful to have Cobain in my life and was grateful to Andy for not putting up too much of a fight to keep my giant baby. Cobain never judged my choices or kept a tally of my mistakes. In a world where I felt like I had once again failed, Cobain was a safe space where I could be fully myself.

The headquarters for the company I worked for was in downtown Seattle, so Cobain and I moved to the big city. I bought us a small brick house in the Montlake neighborhood of central Seattle. It was a quaint, older suburb with a lot of natural beauty. Living closer to the home office, I now planned to go in a few days a week and wanted a short commute so Cobain wouldn't have to be alone longer than necessary. She wasn't used to me being gone during the day.

I knew that if I stayed in Westport, Andy would want to see Cobain regularly, and I couldn't go down the road of seeing him every few weeks. It was selfish, I know, but I also knew Andy would try to talk me back into being with him, and I didn't want him to think that was an option.

This is about the time when the Universe got tired of my bullshit—tired of me dodging the lessons, hanging on to my outdated patterns, and hiding behind child-like behaviors. So, it dropped a new man right in my path. One I couldn't outrun. One I couldn't ignore. And this man didn't just challenge me; he wrecked everything I thought I knew about myself. He tore down the version of me I'd been clinging to and held up a mirror I couldn't look away from—no matter how hard I tried. He was conveniently disguised as my knight in shining armor.

His name is Todd.

The enticing tang of earthy herbs entered my office, waking Lily. I leaned down to the dog bed where she was now stirring and gently cradled her ears. As I smelled the scents of lunch, I glanced at the big gold clock on the wall. Simultaneously, Laura grabbed her belly after it let out a long, monotone growl. She quietly giggled in a way that showed she was trying to excuse her stomach for making so much noise.

I smiled kindly at her and then gazed at Lily, watching her paw at her face, wishing I'd scratch her ears again. Looking back at Laura, I said, "You know, dogs don't care about your past, your mistakes, or how many times you've been divorced. They love you at your best and your messiest—mud-stained sweatpants, ugly crying, and all. You don't have to earn their love. You just have to show up."

I paused for a moment, feeling the words I had just spoken, knowing how long it had taken for me to understand and embody them.

NINE

It was just after noon, and Laura and I were eager to eat the delicious lunch Chef Vincent had prepared for us. Lily was now fully awake, and she sniffed the air as if she were a detective looking for clues. She let out one quick bark as she raced towards the door. I rose from my chair, walked across the office, and opened it for her. Lily bounded out the door, nearly knocking me over with her excitement.

I lovingly watched her dash down the hallway and said, "Well, somebody's sure hungry. Let's make our way to the kitchen and have some lunch before you nearly knock me over, too. " I flashed a grin at Laura.

Laura paused the recording app, closed her notebook, and placed them back in her bottomless bag.

"I thought you'd never ask," Laura answered playfully as she rose out of her chair. She moved so quickly that she knocked over the tote, spilling some of its contents onto the floor. She gathered them swiftly and hoisted the bag onto her shoulder as she made her way toward the door.

"If we ever get stranded on a desert island, I'm sticking with you and that bag. It looks like you have supplies for a month."

"Hey, when you've spent part of your life not knowing where you'll sleep, you learn to carry everything but the kitchen sink. And honestly? If I found a collapsible one, it'd be in here too."

"I totally get that!" I replied.

We made our way to the kitchen, chatting and laughing as we viewed random contents from Laura's bag.

In the kitchen, we sat at the same informal dining table as we had the day before. The large picture window framed the grey, cloudy sky, and drops of rain looked like they had been gently drizzled on the glass.

On today's cabbage green, floral dinnerware, Chef Vincent served us stuffed roasted bell peppers with herbed lentils and cashew cream, accompanied by grilled zucchini ribbons tossed in olive oil and lemon zest. For Lily, he prepared a feast of humanely raised organic turkey and sweet potatoes, with a blueberry and banana pup-scicle to start. Chef Vincent was like a little kid—always eager to serve the desserts first. And Lily never objected.

Over lunch, Laura shared more about her life as a teenager and how being abandoned by her mother and being unhoused for a time affected her life. Laura and I shared a mother wound in common and equally understood how that felt. To my surprise, we were developing a friendship, certainly one I hadn't expected.

After we shamelessly polished off a dessert of coconut chia pudding with berries and cacao dust, we thanked Chef Vincent for his delicious lunch. Laura, along with her emotional support tote bag, excused herself to the restroom. I took Lily out to potty using the mudroom door. I knew Lily would take a quick romp in the mud while she was outside doing her business. I was glad I had a chocolate lab and not a yellow for this very reason: Lily often became filthy. She was born and raised in the rain, and once she was out in it, she always had to shuffle through every puddle she could find along her path.

Once Lily was cleaned and dried off—nearly fifteen minutes later—I found Laura in the kitchen swapping recipes with Chef Vincent.

"Oh, I wondered where you went," Laura said.

She then turned to Chef Vincent and thanked him as she held up a brown bagged meal.

"You're welcome, Laura. When I knew you wouldn't be staying for dinner, I at least wanted to make sure you had something healthy to eat for your travels."

"You are too kind, good sir." With a grin and a dramatic flourish, Laura bowed low as though accepting a royal decree.

Chef Vincent and I both laughed.

Although the rain had stopped, the weather outside was still not ideal for continuing the interview outside. Lily stayed with Chef Vincent in the kitchen, and Laura and I returned to the familiar office. Along the way, Laura mentioned the calming irregularity in the weave of grasscloth wallpaper that lined the hallway. She had an attention to detail that I appreciated.

Once we were both settled back in our chairs, Laura removed the recording app, her notebook, and a pen from her Mary Poppins bag. As she started the recording app, she said, "Okay, tell me all about your life with Todd."

I closed my eyes for a moment, let out a long sigh, and began.

One might surmise that after a third divorce, I would opt for some introspection or at least consider it. Right? Well, growing up with parents who didn't model good relationship skills certainly didn't help me in this area of my life. Without self-awareness, self-reflection doesn't exist. I simply told myself I was just bad at choosing the right men.

If you can believe it, I decided that my method of finding the perfect partner would be manifestation. I was now in my early forties, and I decided that if I just gave careful and more precise thought to the kind of partner I wanted in my life, that would be the answer to finding true love. And yes, if you think I was somewhat delusional, you're not wrong. I was, indeed, delusional about many things.

I told myself that my restart in life would be different this time. I was older and wiser, or so I thought. I believed I could manifest exactly what I wanted in my life going forward. No more winging it this time. I would lay out the plan for myself and stick to it.

Over the next twelve months, and in this specific order, I would earn a promotion, make more money, and become an outstanding tennis player. Seriously, those were my goals at the time. Then, at some point down the road, I wanted to meet a man who met the following criteria: divorced with two younger children, financially stable and career-oriented, loves animals, and enjoys being physically active and social. Not a solid, soul-focused plan, mind you, but a plan nonetheless.

And if you think you were hearing things when I said that I wanted a man with two younger children, you heard correctly. Here's the thing: I actually did want children in my life. It wasn't until I was in a relationship with Andy that I realized I had been hiding my desire to be a mother. I had been so ashamed and consumed with grief and sadness after the failed IVF attempts and the loss of Antin that I retreated from the possibility of motherhood altogether. I gave a quiet death to the version of me who believed I was meant to be a mother.

But grief is a strange thing—it softens at the edges when you're not looking. And, towards the end of my relationship with Andy, I would catch myself wondering if there was still a way to become a mother. Hence, my new search for a man with younger children.

Okay, so my new plan, which included being a highly skilled tennis player, was in motion. I decided to join the Seattle Tennis Club, which sat along the shores of Lake Washington. I was ready to get out and be social. I was used to meeting new people and reinventing myself, and this time would be no different.

On a crisp and clear Saturday in early August, I was invited to play a doubles match with some women at the tennis club on the indoor courts. Throughout the two-hour match, one woman, Danielle, curiously inquired about my dating availability. She told me that her husband was playing golf with an acquaintance named Todd. After the tournament ended that evening, Todd was hosting a party at his house, and Danielle and her husband were going. She insisted I join them. Todd was single. Danielle swore she wasn't trying to set me up with Todd, but I could sense her intentions.

I politely explained that I had just finalized a divorce and wasn't interested in dating anyone for a while. To say she was persistent is an understatement. This woman was on a mission to get me to Todd's house that night. After kindly telling her "no" more than five times during our match that afternoon, I reluctantly agreed to follow her husband and her to the party. I insisted on going separately in my car. At the very least, I wanted to be in control of my exit. Sound familiar? Me, wanting to be in control . . . of my exit, of all things.

As I drove into Todd's fancy neighborhood, the gated community of Broadmoor, the Universe's well-orchestrated plan was coming together.

Todd was, and still is today, the life of any party. His six-foot-two-inch presence filled the room that night. And I was captivated. I had become accustomed to Andy, a wallflower in social settings. Todd is the exact opposite, and it was incredibly refreshing. When we met nearly fifteen years ago, Todd's thick, wavy blonde hair was his trademark. His blue eyes were bright and mysterious. To me, he looked like he was right out of a magazine.

Danielle introduced us, and the first thing I noticed was that I didn't have to carry the conversation. Todd was engaging, chatty, and seemingly interested in getting to know me. I say "seemingly" because he had been drinking all day while playing in the golf tournament, and I honestly didn't know if he was just a good host or if he was truly interested in me as a person. I stayed at his party for a few hours, getting acquainted with some of his friends and neighbors, believing I'd never see any of those people again.

Todd asked me for my phone number when I said goodbye to him that night. I mischievously responded, saying, "Nope, you will have to find it yourself." I was shocked when those words came out of my mouth. Who was I? I drove home, mentally replaying the evening, and then I quietly crept into the house, trying not to disturb Cobain. I felt uncharacteristically hopeful. It felt like my heart was telling me I was in the right place.

About a week later, I received a message from Todd in my LinkedIn inbox. He found me. I felt both impressed and excited. It felt way too soon to start dating again, but there was something about Todd I couldn't dismiss. I agreed to go out on a date with him a few days later.

Like many people, prioritizing romantic relationships over all other aspects of life was another familiar pattern for me. I often placed far too much value on others paying attention to me during many periods of my life. Given the internal view I had of myself—unlovable and unworthy—I always felt shocked when someone, anyone really, took an interest in me. Any interest someone had in me, intimate or platonic, I found difficult to trust.

I was dumbfounded when Todd wanted to keep seeing me after those first few dates. He was a handsome, divorced man with three children. He had a professional career, was financially stable, physically fit and active, loved Cobain, and wanted to keep dating me.

How in the hell was this possible? I thought.

Todd was even okay with it when I told him I had been married three previous times. Was this the man I had manifested? Wow, if so, I'm pretty good at manifestation!

Athena said, *Take it slowly. This is happening way too soon. Get to know him before you rush into anything.* And, true to my pattern, I ignored Athena again.

My house was only a mile and a half from Todd's, and in a city as big as Seattle, it still boggles my mind how I ended up buying a house that close to him in Broadmoor. A few weeks later, after Cobain and I had been staying with Todd at his very large, manicured home, he nonchalantly asked us to move in with him.

Even for me, that offer felt very hasty, especially with three children involved. Hmmm, was this a red flag? I still kept my home and stayed at Todd's place when his kids weren't with him. He slowly introduced me to them over those following weeks, and by late October, I was selling my house. Cobain and I were moving in with Todd.

For our first Christmas together, Todd whisked me away on a trip to Paris. On our second night there, after dinner at a charming restaurant with a view over the city, Todd proposed to me. It was a mere four months after our first date.

In many ways, our romance was beautiful, idealistic, and exhilarating. But the pace at which it was moving felt too much, too fast, too soon. I remember thinking, *Why am I agreeing to get married again, and so soon? This doesn't feel like the kind of thing a rational person does the fourth time around. What am I doing?*

Now, here's something ironic. When I was packing, unpacking, then repacking and unpacking my moving boxes, all within the span of four months, I stumbled across all the self-help books I had bought back in Des Moines. These were all the books I had skimmed hundreds of times. Had I actually read those books and learned how to have more self-awareness, I probably would've also been asking myself some deeper questions like, was I addicted to instability? Chaos maybe? Or did I perhaps need complexity in my relationships to feel stable and comfortable? Lesson learned—skimming self-help books may give you a summary of the information they hold, but it does not give you the insight needed for any real change.

Honestly, all that was missing was a checkered flag and someone yelling, "Winner!" Because even with all the giant, flashing warning signs along the track of my life, I was still flooring it like I was in first place at a NASCAR race—zero awareness, full speed ahead.

What the books contained—I know this because I've now read them all multiple times—were theories and studies on how some people, due to past trauma, low self-esteem, or fear of abandonment, become addicted to excitement and chaos as a way to mask their inner pain. Additionally, the dependence on chaos is reinforced if a child grows up in a chaotic environment or with fractured family relationships. Comfort arises from turmoil, and unease appears in moments of calm.

Learning this could have been an ah-ha moment for me at the time had I made the effort to read the books thoroughly. It's not enough to buy them; one has to also read and embody the knowledge they contain.

I felt a magnetic pull toward Todd since the moment I met him, maybe even before. It was almost as though the Universe had aligned to bring us together. I know how corny that sounds, trust me. I could never explain the feeling; it was just always present. Even our first date and first kiss felt familiar and comfortable in a good way. Yet, an odd underlying tension was often present between us. I could never put my finger on what that was exactly.

Six months after our relationship began, we had an intimate wedding ceremony at Cannon Beach on the northern coast of Oregon. The ceremony consisted of a wedding officiant, Todd, me, and the kids—my soon-to-be step-children, whom I affectionately call my gift-children.

Todd is a loving man. He is loyal and generous, and he is a great provider. He is also excellent at making money. Like Brian, he loves his career, but Todd prides himself on having a good work-life balance. He loves the outdoors, like both David and Andy, and has an active social life. He is a great blend of all three of my prior husbands in all the ways I needed. Todd also has a very assertive, take-charge energy, which, today, I can now appreciate.

I couldn't say that about him early in our marriage. Prior to meeting Todd, my survival strategy required me to exude a more hyper-independent, achievement-oriented personality in my relationships.

Though I didn't know it then, my relationship with Todd started off balance because we were both this masculine type of energy. Todd was displaying the healthier form, and I was showing up in a more harmful way. We were like two rams locking horns—each one stubborn, each one sure they were right. Neither wanting to back down.

I never learned how to be soft, graceful, or truly vulnerable. Growing up, I had to be strong and in control—I didn't have the opportunity to let go and trust. When both people in a relationship are trying to lead, control, and protect, balance rarely exists. The relationship devolves into a constant power struggle rather than a real connection.

Back then, Todd and I both worked full-time. He was in consulting, and I was still in the tech business. When I joined the company, clear back when Brian and I were married, the company was little more than an idea and a whiteboard. They couldn't afford to give me a decent salary at the time, so they gave me stock options instead—more than they probably should have, honestly. The company went public just after I moved to Seattle, and by that point, I had been the VP of Operations for nearly three years.

Todd regularly traveled to various parts of Europe and Asia to meet with his top clients. He was a management consultant at a large firm in Seattle and, at the time, was always toying with the idea of starting his own consulting firm.

Todd shared custody of his kids, who were fourteen and sixteen at the time, a set of twin girls and their younger brother. Depending on Todd's travel schedule, they lived with us every other week and on some weekends. They were busy teenagers, so even when they were at our house, we barely saw them. A year had passed since we married, and although I was developing a friendly relationship with the kids, I kept my distance when it came to the day-to-day stuff. I also tried staying in the background when they were around. I remembered what it felt like to have a new step-parent, and the last thing I wanted was for them to think I was trying to come between them and their dad.

One afternoon, after the kids went back to their mom's house, Todd looked at me, took a breath, and said, "Julie, I have an idea to run by you."

Uh-oh, this can't be good, I thought.

"I've been thinking about how much I travel and how it's affecting the kids. Their schedule with me gets so shifted around when I'm gone, and I hate that for them."

My thoughts now moved to those of anticipation. Was Todd going to say that he finally had decided to start his own consulting business? Did this mean he would travel less? His prospective business partner, Kevin—a highly successful colleague at his current firm, had planned to be the face of their company, at least according to what Todd told me. Todd would work from Seattle and travel only on occasion. Needless to say, I was expecting to be excited for him, for us, for his kids.

"Julie, you know I make more money than you do."

I defensively replied, "Yes. What's your point, Todd?"

"Well, the company needs me to travel more." He began in a monotone voice. "My boss pulled me into his office today and told me about a big, new client in Switzerland that I will need to start supporting. I'll have to travel even more now. And you know that's not what I want to do, Julie. I'm still vetting the idea of starting my own consulting firm with Kevin, and when that happens, I'll be working longer hours but not traveling nearly as much. Long story short, I'll need your help whichever decision I make. Whichever decision we make," he said, correcting himself after seeing my face wrinkle. "You are really good with the kids. And they're so busy with school, activities, and friends you may not even need to do much. And I know they adore you." He paused.

Is he joking? Not much to do? Does he even know his kids? I thought to myself.

"Julie, would you consider leaving your job? You know you don't have to work. I can more than easily support our whole family. Why not just relax and enjoy your life? Then you can be here full-time, and I won't have to worry while I'm away."

I was stunned. I felt punched in the gut. I was all for providing stability for the kids, but they were his kids, not mine. Then came Athena's voice, *It will be okay. Remember to breathe. You'll be okay.* I had heard those words so many times before. But this time, for whatever reason, I softened slightly. I was able to actually listen to Athena, not just hear her voice, this time. I also somehow managed to drown out Slygore's screeching rebuttal long enough to consider that Todd may just have a point.

"When do you need me to decide?" I asked.

"Well, I'd love it if you could give me an answer by the end of the weekend, but if you need to, take a few more days to think it over. I know you'll want to give your office some notice."

With carefully hidden ice in my voice, I said, "Okay, I'll consider it." I turned away from him and shuffled out of the room, leaving Todd standing there by himself. I needed some space after that conversation.

The thought of stepping into the role of part-time mother and having a man provide for me put me into an internal tailspin for the next few days. Luckily, Todd left for a business trip that next morning, giving me time and space to consider his stay-at-home proposal.

It was ironic because I thought I'd always wanted the luxury of not having to work and having enough money that I didn't need to worry about supporting anyone financially. However, now that the idea could actually become my reality, I felt myself becoming increasingly angry. The more I evaluated the situation, the more irritating and complex my thoughts became.

What about my independence? Why should I leave a job? Why should I leave a *career* that I built for myself just so Todd's career can bloom? What if our relationship doesn't work out? I'll be stuck; I won't be able to leave him. Was this my cost of entry to be in this marriage to him . . . to be in this family?

A small part of me knew Todd wasn't intentionally trying to make my income seem irrelevant, but that is how I felt. I just couldn't wrap my head around letting go of something I had busted my ass to build. My career outlasted two divorces. It wasn't just a job; it was my lifeline. I kind of resented Todd for even asking me.

A few days later, Todd returned from overseas, and the kids returned from their mother's. I had made up my mind that I would not leave my job. We would need to figure out another way to make things work.

I was all set to tell Todd, but wouldn't you know it, pizza and a board game changed my mind. Yep! That weekend, the kids had very little on their social calendars for once, and they all suggested we order in and play Monopoly. They suggested it. We felt like a true family that night. The family I had been waiting so very long for. I was speechless. And that's the moment I knew I was going to quit my job.

Before doing so, though, I did share with Todd that I was worried about not having my own "escape" money. That's what I called it. He found my comment strange but not off-putting, nor was he threatened by it. It was as if he somehow understood that I needed a financial security blanket to give me some predictability and a sense of control in my life. I felt a sense of relief when he explained to me that my fully vested company stock was all mine. It wasn't his money, and I could do whatever I wanted with it when the time felt right. He even offered to help me cash it out and reinvest when I was ready.

Feeling a bit more secure with my decision, two days later, I gave my notice to the company I had been with for nearly fifteen years. They tried to persuade me to stay part-time, but my commitment to Todd outweighed their offer. I had waited a long time for a chance to be a parent, and I wasn't about to miss it—even if my role felt small.

Following Todd's advice, I left my nest egg of company stock where it was, hoping it would continue to grow in value. That security blanket—those 10,000 stock shares—eventually earned me enough money to start Girls Rise and Shine.

By giving up my career, I had to trust Todd even more. In those early days, I wanted to, but subconsciously, my body and mind weren't yet willing or ready to do that. Leaving my career meant no longer having a steady, personal income of my own, and that opened up a wound. Sure, I had my stocks, but that wasn't the same. If the company tanked, I'd have nothing to my name. I had to trust that Todd had my back. Trust that he would take care of my day-to-day needs, my medical coverage, my future, my everything. On repeat, Slygore hissed, *If you couldn't trust your mother, how can you trust a man you've known for only a year? Your stupid, and you suck. He's gonna leave you.*

As for Todd, he immediately decided to start his own consulting business. Within a few weeks, they had their strategy and laid the groundwork. A few months later, they gained traction, built momentum, and, within fourteen months, their new company was flourishing. I was proud of Todd. I was also a bit envious.

Throughout this time, Slygore would mutter things like, *Todd married you just so you could help him raise his kids. He doesn't love you. This is all transaction. He's gonna leave you once his kids move out. You're not doing anything right. You're not doing enough. The kids don't like you. You suck.*

The kids were growing up fast, and I was trying to find more and more ways to keep myself busy. Without an income-producing job, I began to feel the need to prove my value yet again.

As I did in all of my other marriages, I suppressed feelings of unworthiness, shame, and guilt and subconsciously channeled them elsewhere. It always felt like I had a button someone could press, and the moment they did, I'd slip into whatever version of me the situation called for, like a superhero without the powers . . . and definitely not the "super" part.

And for the following long four years, that's exactly what I did. I began repeating all the same behaviors and beliefs that were deeply embedded within me, this time with a slightly different spin. I transformed myself into what I like to call the aggressively busy, brooding people pleaser. I attended Todd's business functions, went to lunch with the ladies, took care of the kids when they were at our house, played tennis, went on long walks with Cobain, learned how to plant amazing flowerbeds, painted, jogged, volunteered, tried learning how to cook, started reading books cover to cover, redecorated the house twice. You name it, I did it.

I did most of these things, not because I wanted to, but because I wanted to make Todd and those around me happy. Yet, the more I did, the more resentful I became. I'd hear myself saying, "Sure, I can do that," or "Yes, I'd love to go to dinner with your friends," or "Absolutely, I can run those errands for you." But my facial expressions and body language were not on board. I went well out of my way to satisfy everyone else in my life, often at the expense of my needs. All of this was exhausting!

By this point in our marriage, some of Todd's unhealthy patterns and childhood survival strategies emerged and intertwined brilliantly with mine. We often found ourselves locked in a battle of wills that featured a lack of flexibility and emotional disconnection. We hid this part of our lives from our friends and family. While seemingly happy to those looking in from the outside, our life was in a state of flux most days. Sure, we loved each other, but we were constantly distressed.

Regrettably, Todd's kids were not always sheltered from our emotional immaturity. I'm not convinced we provided them with a healthy model for building and sustaining meaningful relationships. We tried to manage our emotions constructively when they were in the house, but that didn't always happen.

Nearing our fifth wedding anniversary, Todd and Kevin closed on the sale of their young company. We were shocked that such a thing could happen so rapidly. It's virtually unheard of to start a consulting business and, within four years, become so successful that a private equity firm buys the company. But, like I said earlier, Todd is great at making money.

With the kids now at university and Todd contemplating retirement versus another business venture, I needed another project. So, we decided to purchase a beautiful 7,500-square-foot waterfront home on Whidbey Island, Washington. We planned to use that home as our weekend escape and for various holidays when the entire family was together. No longer having a weekly parental commitment, I poured myself into remodeling the house, and within an astonishingly short six weeks, we began to occupy the home part-time.

The speed at which I was moving by this point in my life was absolutely ridiculous. I did more before nine in the morning than most people did all week. Even Cobain gave me the side eye from time to time. Her tired eyes reflected my exhaustion, too. No one fully remodels an average-sized house in twelve weeks—let alone a massive, three-story place two hours away in just six.

Todd even dubbed me "Taz," as in the Tasmanian Devil. You remember that wild, hyperactive, tornado-like cartoon character who would destroy everything in his path. Well, I did not consider that nickname a badge of honor. I hated it when he called me that. Probably because behaving like a Taz wasn't doing me any favors, and I could feel it in my bones. My physical body was on overdrive, my mental body was about to implode, and my emotional body was still hiding in the shadows.

I guess the Universe finally decided it had to get a little louder. It needed another way to get my attention because I had become far too skilled at ignoring all of its little nudges over the decades. Far too adept at dismissing moments where I could've been more present, more alive, more aware—opportunities to slow down in life and become more balanced and centered. Too willing to tune out turning points where introspection and healing could've taken place. I avoided all the opportunities to see the patterns, beliefs, and behaviors being reflected back to me in my relationships.

Todd and I were cooking dinner for Stan and his wife, who were visiting us at our waterfront house. It was mid-August. My eighty-year-old stepmom stumbled up a small set of steps near the scullery adjacent to the kitchen. She ended up with a few scrapes and bruises, but overall, she was fine. About twenty minutes later, Stan fell in the exact same spot. He was also fine, but two falls in the same space within an hour seemed strange. I remember Todd walking over to the steps and inspecting them. He didn't notice anything unusual.

A few minutes later, a fuse blew in the kitchen, and some of the outlets no longer worked. Always hyper-alert for ways to prove myself, I began looking for another appliance to use to test which outlets were still working. So, I did what any quick-thinking, tiny-framed, independent-minded woman would do. I walked briskly into the scullery—next to the small set of steps that had been that evening's tripping hazard—and grabbed the closest thing I could find. I picked up our Hobart kitchen stand mixer. That thing weighed close to a hundred pounds and was sitting right next to a blender a quarter of its size. Why didn't I just grab the smaller blender, you might ask?

Well, I grabbed the ridiculously large commercial mixer because Todd was making homemade pizza, and I thought I was being both helpful and useful at the same time. That's what superheroes do, right? I hoisted the mixer into my arms and began carrying it into the kitchen. More accurately, I attempted to carry it into the kitchen. After taking a few steps, I noticed that my vision was limited to above the chin level. As I began to shuffle the ten feet into the kitchen, the visual limitation prevented me from seeing sweet old Cobain lying on the floor in front of me. Can you guess what happened next?

As I fell forward, the weight of the massive mixer propelled me out and down, saving my face, elbows, knees, and feet from even a minor scratch. Notice I didn't mention my hands. Those were sadly crushed between the slate floor and the flat underside of the mixer's stand. However, the mixer gracefully tumbled forward, leaving a massive dent in the newly painted kitchen wall. That mixer never saw the light of day again.

As I sat on the floor in shock, Todd, probably equally shocked, yelled, "What do I do?"

I rudely responded, "Call fucking 911!"

Immediately after I said that, my brain said, *Look at your left hand.* When I looked at my left hand, which I couldn't feel at the moment, it looked as if a Palermo bull had trampled over it. My thumb was already twice its normal size, and the bone that runs from the index finger to the wrist was no longer connected together but was not yet bleeding. *This is an indication of a seriously deep wound*, I thought. Then, my brilliant brain said, *Hey, you've got another hand on the right side; take a look at that one.* Apparently, for a moment, I'd forgotten I had two hands. My right hand was covered in surface wounds, and my index, middle, and ring fingers were all loosely dangling from the rest of my hand. I'm no doctor, but I knew that was not a good sign.

With shock settling in after looking at both hands, Athena once again spoke to me, *Don't worry. It will be okay. Remember to breathe. You'll be okay.*

Then I heard another voice. This one was straightforward and stern but not mean, unlike Slygore's voice. It said, *Julie, you need to get up off this floor because, in about thirty seconds, you're gonna feel massive pain.*

Everyone in the room must have been in shock because no one rushed over to help me up off the floor. I raised myself up onto my knees and elbows to stand up. Blood began to ooze out of my hands, and I somehow managed to calmly walk out to our screened-in porch, which was next to the kitchen. The moment I sat down on the wooden lounger, a pain that washed over me was nothing I had ever felt before. It was excruciating.

Our island house was in a fairly remote area. The nearest hospital was over thirty minutes away, and the local volunteer fire department was about fifteen minutes away. The first to arrive and offer aid were three people from the volunteer fire department. Their job was to ensure I didn't pass out or die before the ambulance arrived. That's it. No other job than that. No administration of pain meds, no covering of my wounds, no nothing. So now, six people were just standing or sitting around watching me bleed and suffer while we waited for the ambulance to arrive.

For forty-five minutes, I tried to remain present in my body. At that time, I didn't formally know breathwork, but I instinctively started deep, patterned breathing to calm my body, which was clearly in shock. Maybe this was what Athena was talking about all along.

When the ambulance finally arrived, my injuries were stabilized, and I received three injections of morphine. I demanded Todd stay behind with Stan, his wife, and Cobain. I knew the whole process of patching me up would take hours and figured there was no need to waste the rest of their evening.

By the time the ambulance got to the hospital, I was higher than a kite and had the medics cracking up with my lame jokes and other antics. In the emergency room, the X-rays confirmed three broken fingers on the right hand. On the left, I had a fractured radius in addition to another broken finger. The doctors and nurses said they had never seen an adult come to the ER with two broken hands at the same time. One of the nurses, with an odd sense of humor, gave me a sticker for my shirt that said, "You did it!"

After the x-rays, temporary hand casts, additional medication, and what seemed like an entire hospital of rotating nurses' and doctors' assessments were complete, I was free to go. The ER staff called Todd, who picked me up. We drove through a fast-food place where I ordered French fries because, by now, I was starving. As soon as the fries were handed over by the man working the drive-thru, I tried grabbing the bag from Todd. That was a fail. I then tried opening the bag. Another fail. We flashed each other a glance, quickly realizing how challenging the next few months were going to be—for both of us. I couldn't use my hands at all. With my stomach screaming for food, I grasped the fry bag with my stiff, gauze-wrapped wrists and tried to tip the bag into my mouth. This might sound easy, but I was also high on morphine. Another fail.

I was humbled and traumatized on many levels. Todd and I weren't getting along well at all, and as the days went on, I had to become more and more reliant on him for nearly every aspect of my life. I couldn't cook, eat, clean the house, walk, feed Cobain, or do the laundry. I couldn't even wash my own face or body. I felt useless and incompetent. My frustration with my life and with Todd was mounting. He couldn't even put my hair in a ponytail the right way. With Todd as my new hairstylist, I looked like I was trying to bring back the 1980s side pony.

I wasn't used to needing help. Hell, I had built my whole identity around not needing it. I was still reeling from giving up my job all those years ago. Now this? What was the Universe trying to tell me? I felt unmoored again. It was humbling. And maddening.

I thought things like, *How do I prove I'm valuable now? What value could I possibly bring to our marriage as an invalid? What does Todd think of me? Does he pity me? Does he still find me desirable? Is he going to leave me because of this?*

Slygore's random jeers only added to my agitation. *Todd already knew you were worthless. He won't want you now that you're helpless. You can't even pee by yourself. You suck. Go eat worms.*

For nearly four long and tedious months, this type of inner dialogue circulated within me almost daily. I felt like Todd was at his limit with me and our marriage. I had no job. I couldn't take care of myself, Todd, or Cobain. And I couldn't drive a car. What I did have, though, was more guilt, shame, and feelings of unworthiness than I knew what to do with. It felt like the world, as I knew it, was closing in on me.

Six months after I broke my hands, Todd and I went to a costume birthday party for one of his friends. The couple lived in Broadmoor, too, just a few doors down from our house. When we arrived on foot, I stood in the doorway of their expansive living room, trying to match my Western cowgirl costume—a bandana and a leather cowboy hat—with a forced, grouchy, somber expression.

I felt like a stranger to myself. I felt depressed. My now mostly healed hands tipped cocktail after cocktail as I tried drinking enough vodka that night to drown out Slygore's consistent nagging, *You're a failure. You don't know how to be in a relationship, let alone be married. You've messed this one up, too. You're worthless. You better get out soon. You sssuuuuccckkkk.*

Todd and I managed to navigate the after-effects of my accident and stay married, but I still felt disconnected from him. We barely spoke once we entered our friends' house. I was in yet another cycle of negativity bias, where my mind paid more attention to the negative stories than the positive ones. I deeply believed my marriage was making me depressed. Pretending to be mean and grouchy in my costume felt more authentic than pretending to be happy and grateful.

I didn't want to feel any of the unhappy, negative emotions that had been building for years and years, even way before Todd came into my life. I sincerely wanted to feel the same joy and happiness that seemed to emanate from everyone else at the party that night, yet I couldn't. My anger was solely directed at my husband. I wasn't happy, and I blamed him. I was like a broken record, going around and around singing the same words. *Why wasn't he making me happy? That was a big part of his role in our marriage, right? Why am I so unhappy with my life again? Why do I keep picking the wrong men?*

Making matters worse for me that night was Todd's ever-present, life-of-the-party personality. He looked like he was happy and having fun, and that made me even angrier. It's interesting how things change. Five years after meeting him, the very thing I once found exhilarating about Todd was now the exact thing that made me want to throttle him.

I ducked out of the party that night and walked home by myself. The solo, five-ish minute walk gave me just enough time to plan a quick trip to Sedona, Arizona. Exactly why I picked that specific destination out of thin air was not clear to me at the time. I just knew that in Sedona, I could lay out my plans for leaving Todd. Navigating this divorce would be tricky. I needed space and time to figure it all out. I hated to leave Cobain at home. She was now twelve years old, and I knew she didn't have much time left in this world. But I had to go. I was convinced that divorce number four was on the horizon, and I needed a plan for the two of us.

I had never been to Sedona, Arizona, but something about it called to me. It felt like the right place to escape to so I could breathe, reset, and catch my balance before I went and blew up my life all over again. Sedona is nestled among towering red rock formations, breathtaking landscapes, and vibrant sunsets. The town looks like a place where the natural world is alive. It was bursting with energy, beauty, and mystery.

The resort I chose was the perfect mini escape. Adobe-style casitas were nestled deep in the stunning red rock canyons of Boynton Canyon. The landscape was spectacular. Upon arriving, my check-in host told me that the canyon was one of the most spiritually revered and visually dramatic landscapes in the Southwest. "And for those tuned into it," she said, "Sedona offers a sense of something bigger, almost otherworldly."

All I was looking for was peace and quiet from my own mind and an easy way out of my marriage to Todd. I didn't need otherworldly, but I thanked her anyway and made my way to my private suite.

On the second day of my trip, I met a beautiful, soulful astrologer who offered her services at the resort's luxury spa. She had an opening in her schedule and suggested I allow her to read something called my natal birth chart. I was up for the distraction, so I agreed to the reading. As she spoke, I was buoyed by a mix of self-discovery, validation, and revelation. I suddenly felt like I had a deeper understanding of who I was. But how could some cosmic snapshot of the sky at the exact moment and location I was born be so revealing? She noticed how utterly confused I looked and told me to think of the chart as my soul's user manual. It was as if someone had just handed me a mirror, but instead of showing my face, it revealed the deeper architecture of my personality, my patterns, my core wounds, and most of all . . . my potential. The hour-long session left me feeling relieved. Like I wasn't broken. It felt like a homecoming.

But, as I walked the steep hills back to my casita, Slygore was snickering, *Oh, come on. This is way too far-fetched. You don't believe all of that. You suck.* But immediately after his voice subsided, Athena's voice spoke stronger and clearer, *Stop doubting yourself. Believe in who you are. You are stronger than you realize. Look inward.*

The Sedona trip was where I began my deep dive into self-discovery and personal healing. Something remarkable happened during my time there that completely knocked me out of my old patterns and offered me an entirely new perspective on my life. It didn't arrive with lightning bolts or angels. It wasn't some blaring fire alarm or jolt of energy. It was quieter than that—like a sudden, inexplicable sense of presence. Not happiness. Not excitement. But presence. Like I was here for the first time in my life. Within that stillness, I saw my marriage differently, too. Not as something I needed to escape, but as a mirror—one that showed me where I had abandoned myself long before.

For the first time, I realized I didn't need to make any grand external decisions. I needed to turn inward. To do the work. To see if healing myself might change the way I showed up. I needed to do this before I decided to walk away.

For most of my life, I had been chasing love and worthiness through the people around me, trying to fix my relationships, hoping it would alleviate the unwanted feelings inside me. But now, I was starting to realize that no one else could do that for me. I had to meet myself first.

I still wasn't sure if my marriage could be saved, but my experience in Sedona showed me that making decisions from a place of wounding, resentment, or projection no longer served me. Ironically, repairing my marriage with Todd would have to wait. I had to learn how to take responsibility for myself first. I thought that if I did that and, in turn, showed up differently, our dynamic might just shift, too.

No one told me the journey of inner work is incredibly difficult. It asks you to face the very things you've spent your whole life avoiding. Personal growth can sound like "woo-woo" or self-obsession to someone who's never experienced it, like Todd, who is more practical and emotionally reserved.

While I was busy trying to heal my mother wound, set new boundaries, and discover my worth, Todd was feeling disconnected from me and the depth of what I was going through. In his eyes, our marriage was still unraveling. My world felt like a tug-of-war between inner transformation and external disconnection. Todd and I were still misaligned, and now we weren't growing at the same pace or even in the same direction.

At one point, he lost his patience and said, "Julie, it's like we're not even married anymore. Do you remember how you felt when your mom abandoned you? How do you think I feel now?"

It felt like a low blow at the time, but he wasn't wrong. I was abandoning him in a way. I couldn't see the ever-widening gap between us, and I also didn't yet have the skills to reassure Todd that my growth wasn't about pulling away but becoming a better, more present, and fulfilled partner.

That was nearly ten years ago. As you know, Todd and I are still married today.

Our relationship has been both challenging and complex. We've experienced blissful days and horrible days. Days when we wanted to end our marriage and days when we felt wonderfully happy together. We each carry core wounds, deeply embedded beliefs, and coping mechanisms that still affect our relationship today. Our marriage is still hard work, and that's the truth. It's not some fairytale where everyone is healed and happy at the end of the day.

Maybe we will make it, and maybe we won't. But I know that if our story does end, it won't be because harsh, inner critic Slygore was in charge. It will be because Athena—my intuition, my truth, my deepest knowing, guided me here. And that, I've learned, is the only compass I need.

I let those words hang in the air for a moment, giving them space to settle. Laura leaned over and almost paused the recording app, but stopped.

Her brow was slightly furrowed, and she seemed moved by my last comment. She said, "That's rather impressive, Julie. Not because you did, or rather are still doing, your own inner work, but because of the perspective you have on your relationship. You're not clinging to the outcome or what it needs to be or what it should look like. I have interviewed many people who portray their lives as something they aren't. Your honesty has been refreshing."

I said, "I've learned over the past decade that if I don't know, own, and accept the truth of who I am, beneath the roles, the wounds, and the expectations, then how can I truly show up for anyone else? Whether that's Todd, the kids, our program girls, or a random person I just met on the street. Without that foundation, everything becomes a performance. I can't offer real love, kindness, connection, or even my presence if I'm disconnected from myself. I was the poster child for that kind of life. It was like trying to pour from an empty cup, or worse, from someone else's."

"Well, thank you for that perspective and for sharing so much of your life with me. Most people leave out the stuff they're ashamed of when doing interviews like this. I am grateful for your transparency. I know so many of my readers are going to be able to relate to your story."

"You're welcome, Laura. It's been an interesting experience, that's for sure." I checked my watch, making sure Laura wouldn't be rushed if I continued my story. "We have a little more time before you need to head out, yes?"

"Yes, I have about another hour and a half before I need to leave for the airport." Laura paused the recording app and then looked down at the calendar on her phone. "Yes, my flight's not until 8:15 p.m. We're still good to keep chatting. Can we take a quick break first? My bladder isn't what it used to be. And it looks like Lily is ready to go out, too."

I looked over at Lily, who was now standing by the door with her yellow sunbeam stuffie in her mouth. "Yep, that's a good idea. I'll let Lily out and meet you back here in a few minutes."

TEN

While she waited for Lily and me to return, Laura, now back in my office, walked over to one of the lengthy bookshelves neatly arranged on the wall. She had noticed the thousands of books in the room the previous day and now found herself wondering if Julie had actually read them all. The soaring sixteen-foot ceilings made it seem as if the shelves went on and on forever. Two twenty-five-foot walls, covered from floor to ceiling with built-in bookshelves, contained the books. It seemed impossible that someone could not only read but also digest all of the information they contained.

As she looked more closely at each of the titles, she noticed that the majority of the books fell into the category of self-development, self-help, healing modalities, or memoirs by people who were or are on a journey similar to Julie's. She also happened to notice an entire sci-fi section of books, which surprised her. She peeked at those titles as well. As she continued to look, Laura also found titles related to mediation, relationships, yoga, and consciousness. She even took note of a few titles that grabbed her interest, intending to purchase them later when she got home.

She then moved towards the two-story picture window, which resembled a large oil painting of a steel-gray ocean set against a lush green forest. She thought that the view from

Julie's office was just as breathtaking as it was from the deck. Laura noticed the sun was emerging from behind the clouds. The rain had stopped, and she was glad. Laura hated flying in rainy conditions.

"Oh, my goodness. So sorry to keep you waiting, Laura." I said, sounding a little out of breath. "Lily found another mud puddle outside and just had to roll in it. She is obsessed with mud puddles."

"No problem. We still have plenty of time. I was just being nosy, browsing around in your library." Laura replied.

"Well, if there's a book you saw that caught your eye, feel free to take it with you."

"Thank you. That's kind of you. I wrote down a few titles. I'll buy them and have them shipped to my apartment. If you haven't noticed, my bag is already a bit full at the moment. Don't think I can add much else, let alone a book." Laura gestured to her bag as she raised an eyebrow.

"Ah, yes. Your legendary tote. How could I forget that? I think it's basically your sidekick."

Laura grinned as she pulled her notebook and a pen back out of her infamous bag. She turned on the recording app and leaned back in her chair.

I walked across the room, making my way back to my seat, and said to Laura, "I've formed such a love for books over these recent years. I'll sometimes buy a book just because of its energy. I know how strange that may sound to some people. But there is something magnetic about a room filled with books. To me, it's in the way books sit on a shelf, spines aligned like sentinels, each one holding an entire world just waiting to be unlocked. They don't just hold stories or information; they radiate them.

"This is one of the reasons why we have extensive libraries in all of our Girls Rise and Shine facilities—because a library offers safety without pressure. No one's asking our rising women to share, perform, or explain. Their invitation is to simply explore, feel, and reflect at their own pace. Books opened up so many doorways to my own healing, and I wanted our girls to have access to the same opportunity."

I settled back into my chair, and Lily, still damp, stepped back onto her pink velvet bed beside the window. She circled in her bed twice before finding just the right spot. In a stream of filtered sunlight, she was ready for another nap.

As I watched Lily get situated, I noticed the tired-looking, orange-yellow stuffie toy stuck underneath the blanket in her bed. The stuffie had definitely seen better days. It used to be in the shape of a cartoon sunbeam guy and had been washed so many times that you could no longer see the pointy tips of the sun's rays. It was threadbare, sagging, and clinging to the last of its warmth. The words, which were in stitched white raised lettering, were now nearly unreadable.

I smiled broadly as my eyes simultaneously began to well up when I saw the toy. I thought, *It's brilliant that my body can feel two powerful emotions at the same time.* I paused for a moment, then looked at Laura inquisitively. "How about I tell you how Lily came into our lives? That story is the best segue into how the idea for Girls Rise and Shine was conceived."

"Sure, I'm looking forward to hearing how all of this came together," Laura said.

I relaxed into my chair, with my feet tucked up under me, and began the story.

Well, when Cobain passed away about six months after my Sedona trip, I was devastated. I mean, I knew it was coming, but that didn't make it any easier. The thought of never seeing her adorable face again, her greying jowls, or her big droopy eyes was too much to bear. I still get emotional when I think of her. She was my best friend—my anchor. And honestly, she felt like the last real piece of who I was before everything started to shift. Before I began letting go of that old version of me.

And even though Cobain was my dog and not Todd's, he had really grown to love her. The kids, too. The timing of her death was rather poetic, as I was enrolled in a Vedic studies program at the time. A particular section of my coursework that I had just completed was centered around non-attachment, which is the idea of not clinging to outcomes, identities, possessions, or even thoughts.

Non-attachment is the ability to engage fully with life, love, and presence while not letting your sense of self or peace be tied to how things unfold. This is much easier said than done. From the Vedic perspective, suffering comes from attachment to pleasure, identity, relationships, or the belief that anything is permanent.

The perfectly timed class taught me to see that death was a part of life and that it was my ego, my own identity, that wanted Cobain to still be alive. Not right, wrong, good, or bad—just part of the human condition. It's about shifting from a reactive to a reflective way of living. My teacher summed it up with a few short points, saying, "Live with purpose. Act with love. Let go of the outcome. Remember who you are." His words really resonated with me.

Now, this didn't mean I avoided what I was feeling or didn't mourn Cobain's death. Because I did. I missed her greatly. I just mean that by discovering the Vedic approach to life, I radically shifted my perspective on life and the lives of the people I loved. Where modern Western culture often views death as an end or tragedy, the Vedic worldview invites a deeper, more cyclical, and sacred interpretation. I could see the beauty in how Cobain's death opened another door to a different kind of truth for me. I realized how tightly I gripped control, permanence, and my own identity.

At this point in our marriage, our home felt lonely and empty—no kids, no dog. Todd and I were still desperately trying to see if we could, or even wanted to, repair our relationship, and that dynamic often made our day-to-day life together feel even more raw and flat. Todd knew that a part of my heart was missing since Cobain passed, and he, too, was mourning her absence. I know seeing me heartbroken was difficult for him. For months, we talked about getting another dog, but it never went further than that.

It was a rainy day, a little over six months since we lost Cobain, and over a year into my healing journey. At the Seattle house, I opened the side door that led to the yard, which was a space fully enclosed by a fence. We used to use that door only to let Cobain out, so it felt strange to even open it, let alone have a reason to step into that part of the yard. But, standing there, in the huge, fenced-in yard, was a little, scruffy, wet puppy. How she got inside the fence is beyond me. I couldn't tell if her fur was a dark brown color or if she was just encased in mud.

She looked at me with her big brown eyes and with what appeared to be a smile on her long-nosed face. She also had something soft, round, and multicolored in her mouth. She was so damn cute. As I tried to see what she was carrying, I noticed she wasn't wearing a collar, nor did she have any sort of broken leash dangling from her body as if she just escaped from someone's grip while on a walk. I looked around to see if maybe someone was nearby or even down by the road, but saw no one.

In the soaked, matted grass, I began slowly walking on my bare feet towards the dog, trying not to scare her away. She eagerly bolted in my direction before I could even take two steps forward. I mistakenly braced for the impact of a ninety-pound dog versus the wet stature of a twenty-pound puppy and ended up landing backward in the grass with a stinky, dirty, wet dog sitting on top of me. I could now see what was in her mouth. It was Cobain's raggedy, old, waterlogged, sunbeam stuffie that had the words Rise and Shine stitched across the belly. I immediately burst into tears!

Todd, hearing the commotion, came rushing outside to find me buried beneath a strange dog. For a moment, I think he thought I was being viciously attacked, but then he saw Cobain's old plush toy in her mouth, the dog happily wagging her tail, and me half-laughing, half-crying. When she looked up at Todd with those big eyes of hers, he immediately fell in love.

Obviously, we let her in, gave her a bath, and fed her. Todd and I tried for days, weeks even, to find her family or where she might've come from, but no one ever claimed her. That was eleven years ago, and that's how Lily became part of our family.

Now, the other part of the story is Cobain's Rise and Shine, sun stuffie. Back when Andy and I were racing cyclocross, we would often take Cobain with us to the races. She was always very friendly, but many people were afraid of her giant stature, understandably so. Each year, the cyclocross circuit would include a charity race in the schedule. One year, the last year I raced, the organization being supported was a smaller, local version of Big Brothers Big Sisters.

Just before our races, Andy and I were unpacking gear and warming up. An adorable little girl with blond pigtails and big greenish-blue eyes wandered over and eagerly asked to pet Cobain. On her blue t-shirt was a silly-looking, dancing grizzly bear sporting a park ranger's uniform. Seeing the character made me grin. She seemed confident and brave for her age. She also had an oddly familiar swagger. Like nothing was going to stop her.

I looked around for her parents, but she was by herself, as kids often were at these races. Before I could tell her she first needed permission from her parents to pet my dog, she was already hugging and kissing on Cobain. Cobain softly returned the girl's gesture by licking her face, which was out of character for my dog. She was typically sweet and kind but very aloof. Unless she knew you, she would act as if you didn't exist.

As the girl readjusted her purple backpack a few times, I could see her name printed on the side of the strap—Oliva Antin. She then asked if she could give Cobain her stuffed toy. I told her that was very kind of her, but she didn't have to do that. Truthfully, Cobain already had more toys than she knew what to do with and barely touched any of them. The girl insisted and gently pushed the stuffie into Cobain's mouth, and from that day on, it became like Cobain's emotional support toy.

Wise beyond her years, the girl then said something bizarre. "Even the strongest protectors need a little sunshine now and then."

Andy and I looked at each other and simultaneously said to one another, "What in the hell did she just say?" She seemed like some wise old soul inhabiting a six-year-old girl's body. As soon as the girl made her statement, she was gone. It was a strange encounter. Spooky even.

Andy said, "And that's why I don't want kids. They're too weird." I laughed and, in that moment, could see his point.

Later, when Andy and I got home, I had to pry the plush toy out of Cobain's mouth. She had barely put the thing down all day. When I looked at the sun-faced toy with its orange-yellow body, the white letters across the middle read Rise and Shine. As I thought more about the little girl's words, "Even the strongest protectors need a little sunshine now and then." I felt my body tingle and become warm—hot even.

The girl reminded me of someone, but I couldn't quite put my finger on it just then. After a few hours, I realized that she reminded me of me. She even looked like I did when I was a child. I was brave and confident, just like she appeared to be. I also know I had a swagger about me at her age. I remember feeling sassy—like I could take on the world.

Well, this is certainly strange, I thought. I started to chalk up the experience as some weird coincidence. But then I remembered her t-shirt with the dancing park ranger grizzly bear! David and I met at Grizzly's Dance Hall, and he wanted to be a ranger with the Forest Service. That's so peculiar. And the name on her backpack said, Oliva Antin! Antin is the name we gave to the little boy Brian and I were trying to adopt. I'm sure my face looked like it had seen a ghost. My heart was beating out of my chest. *What is going on? This doesn't make any sense. Am I imagining all of this?*

I found Andy out in the garage and recounted to him the whole story I'd formulated in my head. He didn't understand the seemingly strange connections I was making between the t-shirt, the name on the backpack, and the girl's appearance and demeanor. Andy's logical thought process response tried to convince me that I was just seeing things that weren't there—trying to make something of nothing. I knew what I felt and what we both saw, but I let it go. *It was all just a coincidence,* is what I told myself at the time.

Now, fast-forward to Lily finding the sun stuffie in the yard only months after Cobain had passed. Todd insisted—no, he swore on his kids' lives—that he specifically put that toy in a box of Cobain's other personal items for safe-keeping. He knew I'd want to keep that stuffie, her green polka-dot collar, and all of her breed registration papers. I believed him, but when we looked in the box, it wasn't there. Even if Todd didn't put the toy in the box, we still wondered how it got outside. Cobain had it with her in her bed, inside, when she died. The kids were all still off at school, and aside from Todd and the housekeeper, no one else had been in our home. And even if someone was visiting our house, it's not like they'd put an old dog toy, Cobain's most precious item, outside. The whole damn thing was strange. We gave up trying to figure out how it all came to be. In my mind, and I think Todd's too, something greater than us was at play.

Like it was for Cobain, that magic stuffie is also Lily's most prized possession. Lily and the stuffie seem to find their way into the mud more often than I'd like. So yesterday, it was in the laundry, and today, it's here with her, sharing her favorite bed.

As Lily settled into her life with us, Todd was still trying to figure out how he wanted to spend his days. It had been over a year since he had sold his company, and for him, it was still a toss-up between retirement and starting a new business. He was struggling with the decision. While he was trying to figure out that part of his life, I was still completing certifications, taking classes, seeing a therapist, and actively working through my childhood trauma.

It was as if I had a full-time job again. I was busy, but this kind of busy felt different. I was doing all of these things for myself. I wasn't trying to prove my worth or prove that I was lovable to someone else. I was starting to love myself again.

As I became more aware of my ingrained patterns, beliefs, and behaviors and was learning how to shift the ones I had outgrown in adulthood, my relationship with Todd began to improve as well.

Every morning, I meditated and practiced yoga. I incorporated a healthier, plant-based diet to help stabilize my nervous system, improve my mood, and nourish my brain and gut—which is how Chef Vincent came into our lives. For me, eating nourishing food was an essential part of providing the clarity and emotional resilience I needed for all of the deep inner work I was doing. For Todd, hiring a chef marked the end of his five-year-old's diet—no more living on pizza, burgers, and chicken tenders.

I worked with a coach who not only taught me more about my nervous system but also showed me how to regulate it, recognize when I had become stuck in a sympathetic state, and then build my window of tolerance. This alone was fundamentally life-changing for me.

During an intense week-long women's retreat, I was able to release decades of repressed anger, acknowledge and find love for my inner child, and work through some of the guilt and shame I carried about being a barren and childless woman.

Often, I innately wanted to slide back into the old patterns and survival strategies that were familiar and comfortable. The first year of doing my inner work was not pretty, and it wasn't a straight line. It was more like a sideways, multidimensional spiral. I circled back to the same wounds and the same fears, thinking, *Wait, I thought I already dealt with this*. But each time, I'd now see it from a slightly different angle, with a little more awareness.

One of the deepest and most painful layers I kept spiraling back to was the wound I carried from my mother. I didn't call it that at first. I didn't even know it had a name. But over time, I began to understand that much of my self-worth, my relationships, and even the way I spoke to myself were shaped by that deep, early rupture.

The mother wound wasn't just about what happened; it was about what didn't happen—the love I didn't receive. The safety I didn't feel. The day she told me to leave at fifteen still lived in my body like a scar that wouldn't fully fade. But healing also has a way of softening things—not erasing them but expanding how we see them.

Eventually, I stopped looking at my mother through the lens of blame and started seeing her through the lens of humanity. Susan wasn't bad or wrong. She was just lost in her own pain, shaped by wounds she never had the tools to name, let alone heal. I no longer needed her to apologize or to understand. What I needed was to stop carrying her unhealed story as my own. That shift didn't happen all at once. None of this work did. But little by little, compassion replaced my resentment.

I was seeing Todd from a different lens, too, and I was becoming less reactionary with him. I began to notice in my body when he unknowingly said or did something that activated my core wounds. I was learning how to pause, or more accurately, how to attempt to pause, before responding. I say "attempt" because if you've spent most of your life reacting versus responding to a situation, the act of pausing can feel very unnatural—like weakness. It feels like you're doing nothing when your whole nervous system is screaming for you to do something.

Some days, I experienced clarity. I felt lighter, like maybe I was finally breaking free from old patterns. Then, without warning, I would react in old ways, overwhelmed by emotions I thought I had outgrown. I'm grateful that Todd supported my healing journey—even when he didn't fully understand it, even when he felt left out, and especially when it seemed like I was slipping back into an old version of myself.

Todd repeatedly told me to remember that healing isn't linear; it's layered. I don't know if he read that in a book somewhere or simply had that little nugget of wisdom stuffed in his pocket just for me, but I clung to those words often. "Healing isn't linear; it's layered," even became one of the mottos at Girls Rise and Shine.

I also experienced grief, too. Not just over what happened in my past, but over the version of myself who had to survive it. Over all of the time I spent believing I was unworthy, broken, and unlovable.

I occasionally had glimpses of something new. A quiet moment when I'd respond instead of react. When I noticed the activation in me, but didn't follow it. When I paused, breathed, and chose differently. Those moments were gold. They were proof that something in me was shifting, even if slowly.

I was also fortunate enough to have found a clinical practice called Internal Family Systems, also known as "parts work."

This healing framework was exponentially helpful for me in working with Slygore and Athena.

Once I learned how to see, appreciate, and unburden Slygore from his harsh and sarcastic "abandonment watchdog" role, I found more harmony in my life. Slygore would still try to fall back into his old role of my ever-discerning advisor. I would kindly acknowledge and thank him, reminding him that his job had been reassigned. His only request was a fancy title. So, for his dedication to keeping me safe for most of my life, I awarded him the title of Ambassador of Assertiveness and appointed him a Senior Advisor to the Emotional Compass Roundtable.

Slygore's two new jobs were to advocate for my needs with calm strength rather than defensiveness and help me navigate my relationships by tuning into what feels emotionally safe and aligned rather than assuming the worst and armoring up. Even now, Slygore still shows up on occasion, trying to be the captain of my fear. And when he does, I politely remind him that these days, he doesn't need to steer the whole ship for me; he just needs to help me check the weather. That's what I think a large part of healing is about. Not silencing your parts—just giving them better jobs.

As for Athena, the softer, more nurturing part of me, she had spent most of my life greatly overshadowed by Slygore. But the more I healed and the more I connected with my self-energy— that calm, curious, compassionate presence within me—the more I could finally hear and listen to her. Once I created enough safety inside myself, I came to see that Athena hadn't been weak. She'd been the part of me most worthy of protection all along. The one who still believed I was lovable and worthy, even when I had forgotten. And gradually, I began to deepen my relationship with her.

The woman who once hid from herself and others had now stepped confidently forward, asking to be fully seen. The version of me that once survived was now on the way to thriving. For the first time, I wasn't hiding from my truth. I was uncovering it and beginning to live it, and it felt liberating.

I remember thinking, *Every woman deserves to feel this. Not fixed. Not perfect. But free. Free to live from the truth of who she really is, not the version she was taught to be.* That quiet thought became a guiding force—one I wouldn't fully understand until sometime later.

Back then, I had a common misconception about inner work. I perceived it as "fixing" yourself once and for all. It's not. It's about learning to live more consciously in a world that constantly challenges your sense of self. As you grow, heal, love, lose, succeed, and fail, new layers of yourself are revealed. Old patterns resurface in unexpected ways. What you thought you'd mastered might show up again, just dressed differently.

Inner work is less about arriving and more about remembering—again and again—who you are beneath the noise, beneath the roles, beneath the fear. And the truth is, some wounds just don't vanish. They become part of your landscape. You just stop letting them direct your life.

Okay, so back to the stuffie and Todd. Nearly a year and a half after my trip to Sedona, Todd and I found ourselves in a place in our relationship where we could once again have more forward-looking conversations. Over dinner one night, I asked Todd if he had come to any decisions about his career—he was forty-eight at the time. He was still unsure, explaining to me he wanted to do something more meaningful, more influential, or more important with his life. He just didn't know what.

He told me he was tired of consulting. I asked him to tell me what "meaningful" and "influential" meant to him. He said he wasn't ready to retire just yet, but that success now looked different for him, which is why he was struggling with what to do. He said after selling the company, he wanted this next role to be less about recognition and more about impact. He wanted to do something that felt authentic, contributed meaningfully, and left a lasting mark beyond just throwing money around.

When he was done talking, I looked into his eyes and told him that I appreciated him sharing all of that with me. I appreciated his vulnerability and for trusting me to listen. That moment was a huge turning point in our marriage.

I don't know if I saw Todd differently, myself differently, or maybe both. But at that moment, I felt something else shift within me. I could feel how much I loved him—not from a place of needing his approval, but from something steadier. I had compassion and acceptance for him because, for the first time, I was learning to offer those same things to myself.

I wasn't reaching for his validation anymore. I wasn't loving him to feel whole. I loved him because I had something real to give. My love didn't feel like a plea; it felt like a gift. And that changed everything.

Before I could respond to Todd, an image of Cobain and Lily's sun stuffie popped into my head. The conversation with the little girl all those years ago played in my ear. The past connections I made with the backpack and t-shirt resurfaced. And then I heard Athena whisper, *Even the strongest protectors need a little sunshine now and then.*

I just sat there staring blankly for a minute. My brain was intensely trying to put the last misplaced pieces of the puzzle together.

What did all of this mean?

Todd noticed the look of confusion on my face and seemed concerned. He asked me if he'd said something wrong and if I was feeling okay. He waited for me to respond.

I just silently shrugged my shoulders up towards my ears and squinched up my face, indicating that I wasn't really sure what I was feeling.

And then, as if on cue, it was like all the pieces that had been scattered for years suddenly snapped into place. A surge of clarity rushed through me. Not in a gradual unfolding way, but like a dam finally breaking. I didn't figure it out so much as remember something I think I had somehow always known deep down.

I said, "Todd, I know this is going to sound strange. Like maybe I've lost my mind. But I think I know what we are supposed to do with our life together."

Todd's face now looked even more perplexed, but he stayed silent, inviting me to continue.

"You remember the story of how Cobain ended up with the sun stuffie toy, yes?"

Todd nodded his head yes.

To ensure he remembered, I proceeded with a Cliff Notes version of the story, mentioning the t-shirt that had a dancing grizzly in the park ranger gear, the little girl's appearance and behavior, the name on the backpack, and the writing on the stuffie.

He gave me another nod in agreement.

"I think every woman deserves to feel . . . not fixed. But . . . real. Liberated. Able to live from the core of who she truly is, not the role she was conditioned to play by her caretakers, her family, or society. If more young women knew how to access the deep inner work of healing, reclaiming their truth, and living as their authentic selves, the ripple effects would be powerful, both personally and collectively. Think about it. When a woman heals, it doesn't just change her—it changes everything she touches."

Todd listened intently and now seemed more lost than ever, but I eagerly kept talking. He could see my excitement and didn't want to interrupt.

"I think this is what I'm meant to do next, Todd—help other women. I want to create a space where women can have access to all the tools and healing modalities I needed when I was younger. I want to create an environment where emotional literacy becomes the norm rather than the exception. I want to contribute to a society where women learn to trust themselves and their inner wisdom. I want to give women permission to take up space—not through performance, but presence.

"Maybe this is what we were meant to build together. What do you think about starting a nonprofit organization around this type of mission with me? Would this be something that meets your desire to do something meaningful and influential?"

After what felt like the longest pause in history, Todd asked a question—a very valid question. He chuckled a bit, catching me off guard, and said, "I'll give you my answer in a minute, but first, tell me what this has to do with the bear, the girl, the backpack, and the toy?"

"Ah, yes. You want to know how it's all connected. I gotcha." I then continued to lay out the connections, explaining that I might be making these things mean more than they do, but that wasn't really the point. Separately, they might appear to mean very little. But these things collectively felt like reminders, insights really, that my higher self wanted me to notice and remember at a time I was ready to receive them. They were all connected in a way that let me know I was, and am, on the right path for my life and my purpose. What if everything I've been through, every relationship I've experienced, every loss I've endured, every heartbreak I mourned has happened for me, not to me?

I believed the dancing park ranger grizzly character who made me grin was beckoning me to find joy in my life. There was a freedom in the life that David tried to show me. I just couldn't see it at the time. I even met him in a fun, carefree environment, which practically mirrored his lighthearted personality. His easy, playful nature was practically begging me to let go and enjoy my life.

The backpack with the name Oliva Antin was significant because Antin was the name Brian and I chose for our little boy. I think that sign was inviting me to see that the essence of motherhood isn't limited to biology or adoption. It's an energy, a way of being in relationship with the world that nurtures, protects, and brings forth life—not just in children but in people, ideas, spaces, and healing.

My doppelganger, the little girl with the confident swagger, echoed back to me a version of me as a child. I was funny. I was brave, and I was fearless, just like she was. No big dog was going to scare me from expressing the love and kindness I had in my heart.

And the words the little girl said about how even the strongest protectors need a little sunshine now and then held meaning. I now see this as a sign to stop bracing so much. I don't have to be the strong one all the time. It's okay to fall apart. It's okay to feel vulnerable. It's okay to be human. And maybe the energy lives in the sun stuffie, and that is why both Cobain and Lily love it so much. They can feel its vibration.

As for why or how Lily was without a family and ended up in our fenced-in yard with the sun stuffie you swear you put away in a box, your guess is as good as mine. That one's still a mystery to me.   .

I laughed briefly, then stopped talking, allowing time for Todd's brain to catch up. He is a very logical person, and my words probably seemed too mystical or woo-woo for him to digest. Heck, even to me, what I just said sounded more like a page from a self-help fairytale than real life.

I could see Todd thinking, wanting to choose his words carefully. I could tell he was being thoughtful in how he wanted to respond. He gently said, "Julie, I've watched you face things most people spend their whole lives avoiding. None of this has been easy for you—or for me—but I hope you know how proud I am, not just of what you've worked through, but of the woman you're becoming because of it. And it doesn't matter if I believe what you believe about the bear, the name, the girl, and the toy. Because I believe in you. And I believe in us. I always have. Even when you didn't. I'll always support you, Julie, and I'm honored that you've asked me to do this with you. We have a lot to figure out, but let's do it!"

Tears formed in my eyes. I was beyond words. Hearing Todd say he was proud of me was wonderful. I felt so connected to him in that moment. Knowing that I had decided to start living my life from the inside out rather than the outside in and that I had chosen myself, it was like flipping the lens through which I was now experiencing everything: my relationships, my choices, and even my sense of self.

Todd leaned over, kissed me on the forehead, and hugged me. We embraced for so long that Lily, envious, began jumping up on us for attention. She didn't like feeling left out.

Over the course of the following twelve months, Todd helped me define my mission and vision, assisted me in choosing my board of directors, and actually came up with the name. He thought since I had a fondness—that's what he calls it, a fondness—for connecting mysterious dots, we should call the foundation Girls Rise and Shine.

He offered something I hadn't considered. The lettering on the sun stuffie toy, albeit unreadable at this point in its life, said Rise and Shine. Cobain and Lily were females, so in essence, we had four daughters—Todd's twins and two dog daughters—and I wanted to help young women. So, he said he connected those dots and came up with the name. I loved it and thought him even more brilliant.

He took on the heavy lifting—writing bylaws, applying for tax-exempt status, opening bank accounts, handling all of the building logistics, legal stuff, and basic operations. I began doing fundraising, community outreach, and interviewing therapists, coaches, and other people to fill administrative and volunteer roles.

We found experts in their respective fields for various healing modalities to help guide and influence our curriculum. We found partner organizations and businesses to help with materials and supplies. Todd and I worked tirelessly to make my vision come to life.

By the time the opening day arrived, it didn't feel like just the launch of an organization; it felt like the culmination of a thousand promises we made to one another along the way. I looked around at everything we'd built, every form filed, every conversation held, every moment we almost gave up but didn't. I felt something I hadn't felt in a long time: rooted.

Launching the vision for Girls Rise and Shine wasn't about perfection or proving anything. It was about creating a space that didn't exist. A space where girls and women could come as they were—hurting, curious, ready or not—and begin to find their way back to themselves.

I think that's what made it so powerful. Not the size of the building or the polish of the launch but the intention behind it. Every detail was born from lived experience. Every person involved had been touched by healing in some way. And on that day, standing in front of our very first building, sunlight pouring in, I knew without a doubt this mattered.

Since that day, more than 4,000 women have come through our six facilities across the country. The ripple effect of their courage, choosing to look inward for what they once sought outside themselves, is incredible. The effect these women are now having on their families, communities, and society as a whole still blows me away to this day.

Laura didn't say anything right away, but the look she gave me said enough. It held compassion, yes, but also something deeper. Like she saw the courage it took for me to lay my story bare. There was no immediate need to fill the silence. Our presence together was enough. It held the truth that I'd been heard and that what I said matters.

Breaking the silence a minute or so later, Laura said, "Thank you, Julie. When I arrived here yesterday, I was expecting a polished success story, but instead, you handed me something far more vulnerable."

I stayed silent, waiting for Laura to find the words she was searching for. Something in her eyes mirrored my own pain. Something that didn't just hear my story but held it.

After looking briefly at a few of her notes, Laura slowly proceeded to reflect my story back to me in a way only a journalist of her caliber could. With the utmost softness, she said, "What I see in your story is resilience, transformation, and a deep commitment to something bigger, maybe even beyond yourself. You used to search for yourself in other people's eyes, trying to earn worthiness through love, approval, and performance. But now, you hold the mirror and look at yourself from all sides. You still stumble, still soften, and still search. But you do so now from a place of truth. The same mirror that once showed you everything you feared now reflects who you've become—and who you are still becoming.

"And for the girls you and your organization mentor, you offer them what you never had: a steady reflection, a safe place to rise, and a reminder that they, too, are already whole. This is how I'll share your story. Not as a tale of struggle but as a blueprint for becoming. A map for the women still searching, and proof that healing doesn't just change a life—it creates a legacy."

"Thank you, Laura. I know you will tell my story in a way that honors my journey. And as I said yesterday, if my life experience invites even just one of your readers to look more honestly at themselves, then this conversation was well worth our time."

Laura turned off her recorder for the final time. As she began putting away her notebook and pen, she leaned over to give Lily another gentle pat on the head. "You're welcome, Julie. This has truly been a pleasure. I do hope we can stay in touch. Who knows, maybe someday you'll let me write your memoir," Laura said with a sly look on her face.

I shook my head and smiled. I stood up from my chair, inviting both Laura and Lily to do the same. Being respectful of the time, I wanted to give Laura plenty of opportunity to organize her home-on-a-handle tote bag before leaving. Once she had everything collected, including the brown bag dinner, Lily and I walked Laura out of the office and to the front door.

Along the way, we passed Chef Vincent, who checked to see that Laura hadn't forgotten the meal he had made for her, and he wished her well.

Arriving at the door and feeling a layered mix of warmth, reflection, and quiet exhaustion, I hugged Laura and wished her luck with her Born of Fire exposé. Lily leaned against Laura's leg, just as she had done the day before, encouraging one last ear rub from her. I said, "We just spent two days digging through the most vulnerable parts of my life, and yet I'm somehow sad to see you go."

I opened the door to a brilliant beam of sunlight as if the outside world was welcoming Laura's presence. As she walked away, slightly hunched due to the weight of her outlandish tote bag, I smiled slightly. I waved goodbye and wished her safe travels.

To my surprise, she casually turned back towards me and said, "Rise and Shine, Julie. Rise and Shine."

ABOUT THE AUTHOR

Bridget Budd spent over twenty-five years in the corporate world before retiring early. A few years later, a series of life-altering events sparked a spiritual awakening, setting her on a new path. For the past several years, she's been on a personal healing journey, guided by mentors and supported by training as a trauma-informed life coach and holistic health educator with multiple yoga disciplines.

Writing became her passion and creative outlet. With thoughts and emotions deeply intertwined, she writes from the heart. Through story, she invites others to reflect, feel, and heal. *Behind the Mirror* is her first novel.

Through her work, Bridget encourages others to explore who they are beneath the conditioning—and to live from that place unapologetically. She aims to spark meaningful self-inquiry, guide others toward emotional clarity, and help them reclaim the freedom that comes from living in truth—not expectation.

Follow Bridget on social media or connect with her through her website for coaching referrals and other healing journey resources.

Website: bridgetbudd.com
Instagram: instagram.com/bridgetbudd
LinkedIn: linkedin.com/in/bridgetbudd

www.ingramcontent.com/pod-product-compliance
Lightning Source LLC
Chambersburg PA
CBHW071601110726
47908CB00007B/2198